**EVERYONE
THIS
CHRISTMAS
HAS
A SECRET**

ALSO BY BENJAMIN STEVENSON

Everyone in My Family Has Killed Someone

Everyone on This Train Is a Suspect

EVERYONE THIS CHRISTMAS HAS A SECRET

A Festive Mystery

BENJAMIN STEVENSON

MARINER BOOKS

New York   Boston

EVERYONE THIS CHRISTMAS HAS A SECRET. Copyright © 2024 by Benjamin Stevenson. All rights reserved. Printed in the United States of America. No part of this book may be used or reproduced in any manner whatsoever without written permission except in the case of brief quotations embodied in critical articles and reviews. For information, address HarperCollins Publishers, 195 Broadway, New York, NY 10007.

The Mariner flag design is a registered trademark of HarperCollins Publishers LLC.

HarperCollins books may be purchased for educational, business, or sales promotional use. For information, please email the Special Markets Department at SPsales@harpercollins.com.

FIRST EDITION

Designed by Jennifer Chung
Stars pattern © Magdalena/stock.adobe.com
Gift tag art © warmworld/stock.adobe.com

Library of Congress Cataloging-in-Publication Data has been applied for.

ISBN 978-0-06-341286-6
ISBN 978-0-06-342569-9 (international)

24 25 26 27 28 LBC 5 4 3 2 1

Aleesha Paz
For being behind door number 12.

It is a very real danger to the young or to those who have no sense of direction, for many people have wandered off and never come back alive.

—*Arthur Conan Doyle on Katoomba, Australia, 1921*

PROLOGUE

There are quite a few differences between an Australian Christmas and the stereotypical Northern Hemisphere fare seen in most books and movies. For one thing, we don't get snow down under. What we do get, in my specific experience, is more murders.

But before the killing starts (or the recounting of the killings, to be more precise), allow me to introduce myself. My name's Ernest Cunningham. You can call me Ern, or Ernie. I used to be a fan of reading Golden Age murder mysteries, until I found myself with a haphazard career getting stuck in the middle of real-life ones. I'm not a private investigator. I just happen to have a knack for understanding how mysteries tick, provided they follow the rules set out by the classics, of course.

Which brings us here. After having solved two relatively high-profile cases—one, the murders of an imaginatively gruesome serial killer named the Black Tongue, and the second, the public murder of a celebrity—I know exactly where I'm at in my literary canon. So too, it seems, does whichever literary god had the foresight to drop a corpse at my feet at Christmastime.

But I'm getting ahead of myself. It's an honor, in a way, to be part of the esteemed pantheon of the "Christmas Special." A time-honored tradition in which favorite characters don Santa hats, and mistletoe is alluringly hung.

If murder mysteries have rules, so too do Holiday Specials, which the universe has kindly obliged here. You'll find ahead

Santa-fied clues aplenty, and don't rule out characters having to dress up in silly costumes for some tangentially related plot reason, which I will satisfy in a minor turn as Rudolph. And of course, by the end of these things, the detective has to learn the true meaning of the word *Christmas*. So we'll get there too.

I'll remind the cynics out there that the favorites aren't immune to a little yuletide cash grab. Agatha Christie and Arthur Conan Doyle both caved to the whims of the popular desire for holiday murders, though Sherlock Holmes only picks up his single festive case on December 27. I'm writing this all out late on Christmas Day, the rest of my family shipwrecked on couches and beside the pool, glasses of iced white wine sweating beside them, between lunch, dinner or third serves of pudding. On Christmas Day, every meal is the same meal. My point is, I've solved my crimes by the time Sherlock takes his on. Not that it's a competition.

Tinsel-draped as the corpses may be, this is still a fair play mystery. You'll find no hidden clues or unreliable narrators here. My job is to relay to you everything you need to reach the same "lightbulb moment" as I did. A lightbulb moment is, of course, par for the course in these books. In a fair play mystery, we get to the illumination together.

With all that in mind, this whole thing's best treated as an advent calendar. Twenty-four chapters hold twenty-four clues and various bits and bobs that help me with the case. Well, twenty-three clues and a killer, because the best chocolate's always behind door number twenty-four. If you start on December first and take a chapter a day, you'll have it all solved by Christmas Eve, but it's not like I'm going to supervise. Many people like to eat all the chocolates at once.

I'm aware of the irony that this book may be wrapped under a tree at some point. So let's start there. Presents. Seven of them, to be precise, piled under a molting pine. Boxes, spheres, prisms. One is wrapped in newspaper and trussed in twine, one is a big, shiny blue box, and one is so haphazardly sticky-taped it looks like it's been mummified.

I mention the presents to start us off because it serves as quite a handy who's who around the murders in the pages ahead. And the murders this time around might be festive, but they are no less complex than usual: a murder committed without laying a hand; a victim decapitated by a piece of paper; and a suspect, covered in blood, with no memory of how it got on them.

Six suspects. Seven gifts.

Let's open them.

To:

LYLE PEARSE

From:

SECRET SANTA

CHAPTER 1

I didn't know he'd book a magician!"

It's saying something, given my recent experiences include the skinning of my right hand and being stabbed in both the stomach and the shoulder, that suggesting my well-meaning but dim-witted uncle Andy had booked my wedding entertainment might be the thing that led to my demise. Thankfully, a Bluetooth connection and the fact I was driving one hundred kilometers an hour *away* from my fiancée Juliette were keeping me physically safe.

"I know he means well." Juliette sighed, which made the car's speakers crackle. This is another thing about Holiday Specials: sometimes the makers can't afford the whole cast, so several main characters are reduced to voice or pictorial cameos. It doesn't usually apply to books, but here we are. "And I want him to be involved. But couldn't you have given him something a little less crucial than the entertainment? Marcelo's not cooking the wedding cake."

Marcelo is my stepfather, and cooks about as well as Andy chooses wedding bands.

"I thought he'd book a band," I defended. "Hell, *Rylan Blaze*. With a name like that I thought he *had* booked a band." Rylan Blaze was well-known enough that Juliette might have caught me out there, had her knowledge of magicians not stopped at Houdini. "I only found out this morning."

"At which point in our relationship did you think I would enjoy a band called *Rylan Blaze* at my wedding?"

"Our wedding," I corrected.

"Not if there's a magician."

"That'd be the trick then, wouldn't it? The Disappearing Bride." An hour and a half out of Sydney and the road had turned from a freeway to a set of hairpins, climbing up to the mountains at an angle that pushed me back against the headrest like an astronaut at takeoff. "What if I let you saw Andy in half?"

I could almost hear her eyes narrow and her nose crinkle in the way she did when she was still trying to pretend to be mad at me. "Acceptable," she said. "Where are you driving anyway? Reception's terrible."

"I just had to make a quick trip."

"Ernest," she said, and it was all over. I am cellophane around Juliette; she sees right through me. I have no idea how people have affairs.

"I promised I'd go watch," I blurted out. "This Blaze bloke. In the mountains."

"The *mountains*? Which mountains?"

"Blue Mountains. He's doing a Christmas show out near Katoomba." I was up the climb now. The area was a World Heritage–listed national park, and actually a plateau rather than a mountain range; everything around me had eroded into valleys, waterfalls and forests. The eponymous *blue* came from haze that seemed to condense above the treetops, a result of droplets of eucalyptus oil hanging in the air and refracting the light just so. The most famous spot was the Three Sisters—three gigantic rock pillars that stand watching over the valley. People say these pillars have distinct personalities depending on the time of day: from bright happiness to shadowy glowering. If one were to believe they were women personified, perhaps dusk—when the rocky features were overcast and dour—was when they'd been notified of a magic act at their wedding.

"I know it's dumb," I continued. This part of my alibi would hold up if she glimpsed our bank accounts: I had booked a seat at the show. I turned on the hard sell. "This is my end of the bargain: I watch the show, give it a chance, and *then* tell him it's not for us. Besides, poor guy said he paid a—and I quote—*monstrous* deposit, and I promised I'd try to get it back."

"Whoa," she whistled.

"What?"

"I just looked him up. How much was your ticket? How would we afford . . . Does this guy even *do* weddings?"

"I didn't realize he was that big a deal," I squeaked out. My neck was sweating. "Andy knows a guy."

"Riiight," Juliette said, stretching the word in a way that meant she was about to agree but still deciding how annoyed she was. "You staying the night? Seems an excessive errand for December twenty-first."

"Show's at half past eight. Hour, hour and a half tops. I'll skip out at interval if it drags."

The sun was late afternoon lava, a mandarin in the sky. The mountains were a wildflower haven. December's heat had just about done away with the cherry blossoms and purple fists of jacaranda trees, but I still had to turn my windscreen wipers on to scrape away swirls of pink, white and purple petals. The mist in the air was living up to its blue trademark. A glass-floored Cable Car winched its way over a valley, 270 meters high. I'd love to tell you I don't have to perilously hang off it at any stage, but such is my lot in life.

"Erin lives up there, right?" Juliette said, offhand.

The literary detective's pact of honesty is with the reader, not, unfortunately, with other characters in the story. Take, for example, fiancées. Erin is my ex-wife, and the real reason I'm headed to the mountains.

"Does she?" I overacted like I was entering a surprise party I already knew about. Erin's text message, that morning, flashed in my mind. *I need you.* I'd ignored it and the following voicemail for a few hours. But curiosity condemns both felines and Cunninghams. I was packing an overnight bag before the desperate, whispered recording had even finished.

"We could have hand-delivered her wedding invite, then." Juliette interrupted my memory. "Damn."

Yes, I'm cruel to sully Andy's good name as a cover for my trip. But Andy, a former horticulturist and now part-time detective hobbyist, has interests in the following order: lawnmowers, trains, amateur magic, and improv theatersports. Which means he is difficult to sully any further than he sullies himself. Given Andy's involvement was as convincing an alibi as I could muster for purchasing a ticket to Rylan Blaze's magic show, I didn't feel too torn up about it.

"We can spring for a stamp. Besides, it's Christmas week. Erin's probably too busy to meet up," I said, rolling into the parking lot of the place where we would do exactly that.

Juliette and I said goodbye as I switched off the engine. The heat was baking, the tar binding the bitumen gooey, and the humidity was like Jupiter's gravity, the oppressive type that bears on you heavy enough to shorten you an inch. We were in the middle of a conversation-stopper of a heat wave, by which I mean that any chat in an Australian summer is merely a pin pulled on the hand grenade of someone saying "Hot out, isn't it?"

Half the parking lot was in a kaleidoscopic wildflower carpet, ground to paint as I walked over it. I hunched over a little as I hurried across the yard just in case I was spotted. After solving two murder sprees I was now, much to my annoyance, a minor celebrity, and while this place was not somewhere anyone would want to be seen heading into, if someone caught a photo of me here, I knew there'd be some kind of story. A place like this, with an ex-wife sitting behind a locked door waiting for you, is not a place to be papped. The last thing I needed was another tabloid article by Josh Felman, chronicler of reality star divorces and, recently, my investigations. I suppose he's my Watson. That is, if Watson was out to discredit Holmes, and wasn't a particularly great speller.

The waiting room was dispiritingly busy. Small town meth-amphetamine crisis represented in the clientele. The chairs were cheap, hard plastic and I stood in line instead of taking one. A sad spindly Christmas tree leaned in the corner, made impressive by the fact that it seemed to have wilted despite being made of plas-tic. Limp tinsel couldn't bring itself to sparkle under fluorescent ceiling lights. This was an odd place to try and inject Christmas cheer into: no one was coming in here with their families.

"Erin Cunningham," I said when I reached the front, acciden-tally giving my surname instead of Erin's since-reclaimed one. "Er, Gillford. Sorry."

The lady flicked through sheets of bookings. She seemed to have trouble finding Erin.

"Help me out," she said. "We have a couple of wings."

"I expect she'll be in a holding cell," I said. "She's just been charged with murder."

ERIN

CHAPTER 2

Katoomba's police station either had a very comprehensive or a very lax understanding of the law, given how quickly they put me in a room with an accused murderer. I was slightly disappointed: I'd expected obstruction and had prepared a treatise on how someone in custody may invite a lawyer *or* a friend to consult, but there was no call for my recent education at Google University.

It wasn't quite an interview room nor quite a jail cell: alongside an aluminum chair was a wire-framed bed with a tortilla-thin mattress and a blanket so threadbare it would classify as indecent were you to wear it. The door was just a regular door, painted a horrid bile-green, not a set of bars. Erin wasn't cuffed, she was sitting on the bed.

Her hands still had blood on them.

Don't get the wrong idea: she didn't need a napkin. Her hands weren't dripping with it. But her palms showed incriminating dull pink skin and brownish black under uncleaned fingernails. Her eyes were red rimmed too. At first I thought this was anguished rawness, but a closer examination revealed a dry and flaking crust like cheap face paint. Blood there too.

Her voicemail had given me certain details, but now I was able to construct a full image. Erin, asleep in bed. In my mental reconstruction her lips are partly open, bottom teeth showing: we've been divorced for two years, separated for longer, but I remembered her peaceful, sleeping face well. Sunlight slices the room. Maybe a curtain flutters. I've never been in this bedroom so I'm making up the details of a clichéd posh suite. Erin's new partner, Lyle, was head of the Pearse Foundation. In a word: loaded. Erin wakes. She stretches, eyes still closed, and then rubs her eyes with two balled fists. She stops. Something is on her face. Her nose twitches as it registers the thick, metal stench. She opens her eyes and looks down at her hands.

In real life, Erin launched up and hugged me, first squeezing my shoulder blades tight but then patting down my back as if to check I was real. I told her, even though I didn't know if it was true, that it was all going to be okay. Eventually, she pried herself off me and sat on the bed. I took the chair.

She held up her hands: "Caught red-handed, huh?"

I could tell she'd practiced this. She'd picked a tone that she thought would best disarm me, remind me of the Erin Gillford onto whose bloodless finger I had once slid a ring. *It's still me*, she was saying. I could see the grief and the tiredness underneath the act though.

I mustn't have replied fast enough, because she said: "I'm sorry you had to come."

"You knew I would."

"I didn't know who else to call." Her tone was an apology.

"Marcelo's a lawyer, remember. Just in case you get in"—I looked around the room, then back at her pink hands—"*real* trouble."

"I need *you*, Ern," she said, just like her text message had. "Marcelo's all shouting and Latin. I don't need to buy time on a technicality. I need someone to solve this." She paused. "Juliette was okay with you coming?"

"I, uh," I stumbled. "I didn't tell her. She doesn't like it when I get involved with . . . extramarital murders."

I am well aware that lying to one another had caused the derailment of my marriage to Erin, and this was not a good start to my upcoming one with Juliette. But confessions are like morning gym sessions: you have a finite window to commit to one and it gets harder to summon the courage once you miss it.

Erin gave a mutated hybrid of a hiccup, laugh and sob, and pulled at the blanket, which gave up a thread that was probably a quarter of its remaining warmth. I noticed her hair, shorter than when I'd last seen her, cut to her jawline, was also clotted together in ominous dark clumps. When my focus returned to her face, I saw that she was staring intensely at me. Her eyes were bloodshot as well as blood smeared.

Her aloofness, I realized, was less about setting up a persona for me, but genuine apathy in the face of too many emotions to choose from: fear, grief, maybe guilt, weariness, sadness, and, of course, anger.

"They won't let me shower." She held out one of the dark tendrils of hair with a grimace. "Or pick under my nails. Evidence."

"I liked Lyle, he was good for y—"

"You don't need to do that."

We sat in a silence as comfortable as the bed: not very. I checked the time. 6:30 p.m. Rylan Blaze's show was in two hours. If it seems odd that I'm jonesing to make this magic show on time while looking into a murder, I'll fill you in. Lyle's foundation was producing Rylan's show: everyone who worked for him would be at the theater.

"Hot out, isn't it?" I said eventually.

"You haven't asked me whether I did it or not," Erin answered.

"Do I need to?"

For the first time, the corner of her mouth twitched into a genuine smile.

2

RED-HANDED

CHAPTER 3

"I'm not going to lie to you, Ernest. I know that's how you like to do it. So, the honest detective meets the honest suspect. And I want you to know, right at the top, that I *know* how all this sounds. Once I give you all the facts, of which there are frustratingly few, you'll realize I'm asking you to solve a jigsaw puzzle with only half the pieces."

"The facts will do just fine," I said.

"I went to bed around 10:15 p.m. Lyle was only a couple of minutes behind me. I'd like to say we read for a bit, pass ourselves off as intellectuals, but that would be a lie, so I'll admit that our books, well my book and his AirPods—he's into audio—lay dormant on the nightstand and we did what every adult couple does: we scrolled on our phones until we fell asleep. That was probably about half past 11:00. I woke up once during the night and went to the bathroom in the ensuite. I didn't check the time. Temperature was still cooking though."

Normally I might have been suspicious that the story was so specific, but I remembered that she'd probably spent most of the day going over the details with the police, and then again in preparation for telling me. By now this was a practiced story.

"I woke up at 7:45. The sun was up, brutally hot. My alarm was set for 8:00 a.m. but I'm usually naturally ahead of it. Lyle's spot in the bed next to me was empty. That's not uncommon. He's an early riser." Her next sentence was identical to the one she left on my voicemail, down to the quiver in her voice: "I rubbed my eyes. And that's when I felt something. At first I thought it was just crusty-eyed sleep, but then I realized it was on my hands too. And then the smell, oh god, the smell. My hands, the sheets: they were covered in blood.

"I screamed. Just sat there and screamed blue murder. I didn't even think about Lyle, I'm ashamed to say. My gut reaction was that the blood was my own, that someone came in and sliced me up in my sleep for whatever reason, and I had just woken up for the last seconds of my life. But I didn't feel any pain, and I checked myself for bleeding but couldn't find a wound. Only then did I realize that the blood on my hands might not be mine.

"As soon as I left the bedroom, I saw the knife at the top of the stairs. It looked like one of ours, from the block in the kitchen, but I couldn't be sure in the moment. It was bloodied to the hilt. I didn't touch it." She blinked away the memory. "There were drips of blood down the stairs."

"Or up," I interjected. "It's subjective."

Erin's eyes narrowed. "Is that a technique?"

"Huh?"

"Interrupting someone. Is it supposed to throw off any pre-rehearsed rhythm? To trip up a suspect?"

"Would you be offended if it was?"

She weighed me with her eyes. "No," she said. "All I would think is you've rather improved at this whole detective thing since last time."

I'll pause here to recall the adage that it takes ten thousand hours of effort to perfect a skill in any discipline. I figure it applies to detecting as much as it does, say, piano. That is, of course, a lot of dead bodies, so I'd hope to play Chopin before becoming that practiced a detective, if only for the required victims' sakes. If you're keeping track, I solve Lyle Pearse's murder on Christmas

Eve morning, so whack sixty hours onto my tally. I hope I never meet a ten-thousand-hour murderer.

"For what it's worth," I said to Erin, "I genuinely was assessing whether the blood was dripping *up* the stairs by someone carrying and dropping a knife, or *down* by, say, a victim who had taken the stairs after they'd been stabbed. Whether Lyle was stabbed up or downstairs might be important. But"—I leaned in conspiratorially—"thanks for the compliment. So you were following the blood . . ."

Erin examined me. When she spoke next, there was a cautious distance in her tone that hadn't been there before. What I'd really just asked her was whether she'd been holding the knife. "I followed the drops"—she raised an eyebrow—"whichever way they were going. Downstairs was where I found . . ." She sniffed. "Well, you know what I found."

"I know what you found, but I need to know what you *saw*."

She swallowed thickly, and held a long blink. I could tell she was doing her best to give me the facts but keep the memory back. I'd seen enough dead bodies to know the scenes stay on the back of your eyelids forever.

"Lyle was dead." Her tone was flat, like the creepy possessed kid in a horror movie whose tongue is not their own. "He'd been stabbed. A whole bunch of times. Stomach like a dropped birthday cake. There was blood everywhere. He'd written . . . well, I guess it's a message, but it will sound stupid if I say it so you'll just have to see it for yourself. I panicked. Texted you. Then rang, left a voicemail. Then I called the police. They'll tell you that call was at 7:52 a.m. They got there before 8:00. I was still crying when they led me out of the house, didn't even realize they'd arrested me until I couldn't get out the back of the cruiser. They brought me here. Questioned me. Took prints. Samples. And I've been sitting here ever since with my partner's blood up to my wrists because they took away the soap just in case they need my hands again." She was worked up now, the words slipping over each other. The tears she'd been holding back burst out and skied trails through the dried blood beneath her eyes. She held up her hands. They were shaking. "I'm trying to be calm. But ever since the murders we survived on the mountain I can barely eat without thinking about the corpses, the stench, their faces, so not washing my hands is torture for me, and now they're going to send someone in to cut off all my hair. Apparently it's evidence. And after all that, after they took his body away, they gave me the phone number for a cleaning service. Did you know that? If someone bites it on your property, once the police collect the evidence and take some photos, they sign it off and hand it back to you, bloodied and trashed, and basically say *good luck* with a bucket and a mop. And thank God, thank *someone*"—she came up for air—"that you're here."

I switched from the chair to the bed beside her and rubbed her back with one hand while she got the last of her tears out, hoping she wouldn't notice that I was also doing some quick scrolling on my phone. "You did well getting that all out," I said. When her shoulders stopped shuddering, I ventured: "Can I ask a few questions?"

She didn't look up, but her lank hair gave a little shift upwards then down.

"Was Lyle in the bed? When you went to the bathroom during the night?"

"I don't know." She sat up. "I wish I did, but Lyle's bed is bigger than my first apartment. Sometimes I feel I should send him a postcard from my side. And I don't tend to turn on the bedroom light in case it wakes him. I did flick the ensuite light but it was busted, didn't come on. So I went in the dark."

"So," I summarized. "It's dark. You don't know the time. And you don't know if Lyle was in the bed or not. You weren't kidding about the missing pieces of the puzzle. Had you had anything to drink before bed?"

"You mean, was I drunk?"

"No. I mean anything at all to drink."

"I had a glass of water and a hot chocolate." Her brow furrowed. "Why?"

"This is when it pays to have history with the detective. Assuming you haven't changed your routine since we were married, the hot chocolate is currently three-quarters drunk on the bedside table. You drink it just before bed and never finish it."

"Seems an odd time to score points off our marriage flaws, Ern. If I half-finish hot chocolates, you half-finish—"

I held up a hand. "We don't need a sledging match. Fluids take about three hours to trigger the urge to urinate. But chocolate is a diuretic, which means it makes you need to go *faster*. So, if you drink hot chocolates the way I remember, and we put your bladder on the low end of that urgency spectrum, it's a reasonable assumption that if you went to sleep at half past 11:00, you were going to the bathroom at about 1:00 to 1:30 a.m."

Erin looked at me like she didn't recognize me. "Jeez, Ern. You really are some kind of detective these days. How'd you know that?"

"I Googled it while you were crying." I'm not a practiced enough detective to spout such obscure facts. But ten thousand hours hasn't got jack on smart phones.

Besides, this is my third murder case: it isn't enough to do the grand showdown reveal at the end anymore. When you're in a series, the detective has to prove their worth early on with a little bit of inspecting razzle-dazzle. The man in the coffee shop is having an affair because he has a brand-new gym key on his key ring, that kind of thing. It's how an author builds a reader's confidence in the detective and, in real life, it's how you build confidence with a suspect. This is what I'm doing here, not only by quick-thumbed Google searching, but also in laying a series of trap questions for Erin to fall into. At the moment, it was going exactly as I'd hoped. She was walking into every one of them.

"Okay." I pushed on. "So 1:00 to 1:30ish in the morning you get up, go to the bathroom. The light doesn't work?"

"No."

"And then back to bed?"

"Yes."

"You said it was still hot?"

"Stonking. I splashed my face in the hope it'd cool me down."

"So, if Lyle had been dead a while, given the heat, you might have smelled it. Even upstairs."

"Maybe," she agreed.

"I'm thinking there's a chance that, after you went back to bed, someone came and put blood on your hands?"

She shook her head confidently. "I know it's not scientific, but I'm not that heavy a sleeper. I would have woken up if someone had touched me." She looked forlornly at the lumpy bed. She wouldn't sleep here.

"I remember you're easily disturbed. But, for argument's sake, you didn't wake up when Lyle left the bed."

"Yeah, but if somebody touched me—"

"Point taken. You still listen to white noise when you sleep?" I asked. "I never understood why you find traffic relaxing."

"It's called *Tokyo Railway in the Rain*, not *Monday Morning*

School Run. And it is relaxing, thank you very much. More so than *Jailhouse Clank*, which I'll give a run tonight."

"Skip to the morning. I assume you didn't touch the knife?"

"Of course not."

"But it'll have your DNA and fingerprints on it, right? If it's from your kitchen."

"Yeah," she conceded. Then scratched her forearm. "I mean I *think* it will. I thought I saw a knife missing from the knife block, but it's kind of a blur. I was too busy looking for—"

"Wait."

"Huh?" She seemed rattled.

"Nothing. Just interrupting you."

Her eyes narrowed. "What *are* you up to, Ern?"

I breezed past her comment. "What were you looking for?"

"My phone. To call you."

"And you called me first? Before the police? 7:45's when you wake up. 7:52's when you called them. You know they'll be interested in those seven minutes. And they don't like being second."

"Yeah." Her shoulders sunk. "I know it's a mistake. I acknowledged that to the police. I should have called them first, but . . . I don't know. It takes me seven minutes to decide what tea to make. I'm sure as hell allowed seven minutes to process that my boyfriend has been murdered. Besides, you ever tried facial recognition to unlock your phone when hungover? Try being covered in blood."

"You still called the police second."

"I thought that maybe someone was still in the house. A text seemed safest to start. Besides, if I was next . . . I just wanted to say good—" She cut herself off. Guilt rose in my chest. That morning, I'd looked at the text, folded it away from Juliette's eyeline, and let the following call go to voicemail. *I need you.* I didn't really know the procedures on an ex-wife's messaging those three words, but I figured one of them is to not listen to the subsequent voicemail in front of your new fiancée. I'd put it off until the afternoon, when I'd immediately realized the gravity. I was glad she'd trailed off. I didn't think I could stomach hearing that I might have been the last person she'd texted, with the knowledge I'd ignored it.

I pushed on. "You didn't give CPR? Touch the body?"

She shook her head. "I was in shock. I don't know how to describe it. And he was so clearly"—her voice hitched—"well, you know."

"You didn't make sure? No finger on the pulse? No breath check?"

"I just told you I was in shock. And the state of him. When I could, I called you, then I called the police. Then I sat and waited."

"You said he left a message?"

"Not really."

"A suicide note?"

A shake of disagreement. "Like I said, you need to see that for yourself."

"Okay," I said.

"Okay?"

"I think I have enough detail."

"So, what do you think?" She summoned a sad smile. "Reckon you can solve another impossible murder?"

"I think," I said, standing, "your story sucks."

3

1:30 A.M.

CHAPTER 4

You know as well as I do that this story makes you look guilty as hell," I said. Erin's mouth was opening and closing soundlessly as she oscillated between disbelief and outrage. "There are holes all through it. And it's four days from Christmas. Police will want a fast wrap-up. You're a ready-made black widow."

"This is . . ." She pushed past me and knocked on the door. "Hello! We're done here." She turned back to me. "*Unbelievable.*"

I pressed on. "I gave you options to make the story more plausible. If you'd suddenly remembered seeing Lyle in the bed, for example, you would have a better timeline. If someone had put blood on your hands while you slept, we could look at a framing, but you insist you are a light sleeper. You admit you didn't try to give him CPR or stem any bleeding, or touch the body at all, which is a perfect excuse for being covered in his blood. I set you up softball after softball to smash out of the park, and you declined every single one of them and stuck with the *worst* version of the story. Even when I tried my less-subtle-than-I'd-hoped interruption technique to try and throw off your rhythm, you stuck to it."

Her eyes narrowed. "I knew it."

"The point is, there is nothing in your recounting to refute the bizarre conclusion that you violently murdered your boyfriend and then went back to bed. So yeah, your story sucks. And that's why I know you're telling the truth."

A sergeant had opened the door. She had a December aura about her, relaxed shoulders and an unironed uniform: clock-watching until the end of the year. It was past 7:00 now. I had an hour and a half before showtime. I held up a finger, asking for another minute.

Erin was crying and laughing at the same time. "How dare you use me as a cliff-hanger."

"I needed to see how you'd react," I said. This was mostly the truth. I was also thinking it'd be a great end to a chapter as I was doing it. I could have, probably, used less severe wording. That's part selfishness. But it's also what helps me solve the crimes: imagining I'm writing it out for you, whoever you are, so you can solve it too. It helps order the information. On that note, I know it's not very Christmassy yet. We'll get there.

"You'll have been waiting for the indelicate question of money—" I began.

"We're not de facto." Erin shook her head. "Lyle's will spreads his money across various charities, the lion's share going to the foundation. I don't believe I'm in it at all. In fact, I don't think any individuals are. He doesn't have kids."

"At least you're in the clear for motive."

Erin took my hand, squeezed it tight. "Say you mean it. Please. That you think I couldn't have done it? Not because of"—she waved her free hand—"tricks and questions and games, but just because you know me. I'm innocent? You know I couldn't do this, right?"

It was a surprisingly desperate plea. *I'm innocent?* A question, not a statement. For the first time, it felt a little off. Yes, I'd lived with Erin, and loved her, and I did *know* her. Or at least I thought I did. She wouldn't be the first member of my family to have killed someone.

I gave her as reassuring a hug as I could muster. But, just like her, I could only offer a question mark in return. "Anyone who sticks with a story this bad has to be innocent, right?"

4

BAD ALIBI

CHAPTER 5

One of the great annoyances of unsatisfying crime novels is when, after the killer is revealed and the murders replayed, the movements of the villain, on reflection, seem geographically inconsistent. This is most common in slashers, when the murderer must both be featured prominently in group scenes *and* pop up to attack unsuspecting teenagers as soon as they split off. We've all seen the slow walk outpace a college athlete at full sprint. And that's not to mention the time it takes to change into a full-length black coat and ski (or Santa) mask. That's the real tarnish on realism: surely the killer is simply the one who's carrying around a backpack with a change of clothes.

Josh Felman seemed to have mastered the teleportation required of many a literary villain. A journalist's nose is one thing, but the places this guy pops up astound me. Recently, I'd contested a parking ticket in local court, and he'd accosted me on the front steps, thinking my being down at the courthouse must involve a trail of blood and body parts instead of a disagreement over a signpost that had so many time zones on it, it may as well have been the UN. And no, that joke did not go down well with the judge.

The point is, I had no idea how Felman had managed to get to Katoomba so quickly, let alone how he knew I'd be there. Nonetheless, his fluffy microphone almost decapitated me the moment I walked out the police station doors and, once I registered what was happening, I almost wished it had.

Now, don't get me wrong, I don't mind journalists. Clearly

documentation is my thing. But Josh Felman is a truffle dog of a journo who prides himself on being the nearest to the stories rather than the best at reporting them, and whose mileage is higher than his paycheck. I say this with only slight bitterness: his series on me is called The Slapdash Sleuth. Annoyingly, it's been his most popular recent column, and so here we are, with him chasing me around the mountains.

Felman does everything himself, so he was, as usual, kitted out. He had a little shoulder-mounted GoPro, an SLR camera with a surely compensatory-sized lens hanging around his neck, and a backpack filled with all kinds of whirring devices, out of which protruded a boom microphone on a hinged arm that arced over his head and in front of him. A pair of headphones snaked from his TARDIS rucksack, but he only ever had one earbud in, the other flapping by his neck. Everything was khaki, from his hiking boots and socks, pulled up to mid-calf, all the way to his safari-style kerchief. His fisherman's vest and cargo shorts were bristling with zips. He looked like a cross between a paratrooper and a one-man marching band. Which made sense because, to him, journalism was war.

"Leave me alone, Josh," I said, swatting away the microphone. He was, as always, sweating and out of breath. His thinning red hair was glued to his head like a child's art project. Felman's entire personality was *I've-just-arrived*.

"Ernest! Buddy!" He fell into rhythm half a step behind me. His tone was over-the-top friendly. I find it hard to tell whether Felman is delusional, and actually thinks we're friends, or whether he's being ironic. I kept walking. "What'd I ever do to you?" Josh complained.

"'Slapdash Sleuth Can't Solve Parking Puzzle,'" I said, without looking at him.

He barked a laugh. "Oh, come on. That article was an indictment of the draconian parking systems. It wasn't a *character* assassination." He did his best impersonation of offended. "I would never."

The microphone swung around in front of me again. I slapped it back and quickened my pace.

"Is she innocent?" Felman hurried along beside me. Due to the weight of all his gizmos he looked constantly at risk of toppling forward.

"No comment."

"You were married to her. You must know if she's capable—Oh! Did *you* ever feel like *you* were at risk? While you were married, oh!" He shook his head. I imagined his brain was a snow globe of clickbait phrases, the letters all jumbled in color and typeface, as if from ransom letters, and Felman just went with whatever landed first. "Would you say you had a *narrow escape?*"

I whirled around to face him. It took him an extra half second to stop given the momentum of his kit. "Don't you dare write something so salacious. Erin's just lost the man she loved. That's all there is to it."

"Lyle Pearse. Yes." I realized too late I'd done exactly what Felman had wanted me to do, stopped to correct him, so now he had a conversation going. "Local philanthropist of the Pearse Foundation. Murdered. You've met him?"

"Once or twice. Twice." I tried to be as accurate as possible, in case I was quoted. "Family barbecues, that kind of thing."

"You like him?"

"I didn't know him."

"Did you resent him? He was dating your—"

"Is this really where you're going with this?" I clicked my car keys, hoping that the orange flash of the headlights would be enough of a hint that I was fed up, and turned away. "See you sooner than I'd like, I suspect."

He put a sweaty hand on my shoulder. "You don't want to see the photos?"

I hesitated. "What photos?"

"Do you dislike Lyle Pearse? For screwing your—"

"What photos?" I grabbed his overhanging microphone and pulled. I'm not particularly strong, but the combination of physics and angles meant that Josh was easily unbalanced. I'll admit I got some satisfaction from his pinwheeling arms.

"Let go! That's a two-thousand-dollar microphone. Leggo, man! Christ, fine . . . the *body*!"

"Pearse's body?" I let him get his balance back. He folded his microphone in, dusted and cradled it like it was a child I'd just berated. "How'd you get those?"

"Crime scene photographer's off to Bali for the holidays. I know a guy at the airline, bumped him up to business class—"

"Show me."

He waggled a finger. "You talk, I show."

I sighed. "No. I don't resent him. I thought they made a good couple. Like I said, I only met him twice, but I admired the guy. Doesn't everyone? The Pearse Foundation does amazing work."

I meant this. Lyle Pearse was a retired-actor-cum-philanthropist who spent almost all, it was reported, of his small fortune on the foundation, which helped down-on-their-luck young adults recovering from drug addictions. Lyle had never touched a drug in his life, even among the temptations of Hollywood, but at the peak of his career, his brother, back home in Australia, had overdosed on cocaine that had secretly been cut with heroin. Lyle threw his career in almost overnight, leaving a much-prized turn as a popular superhero behind. He'd started the foundation soon after. His method was unique: he believed that the real key to long-lasting reform was igniting a fire, a passion, inside people. That passion could drown out the temptations of addiction. And he thought that fire could be brought about by one thing: theater. The philosophy's a little gamey, but credit to Lyle, it seemed to work. And yeah, I know a little too much about him. But who doesn't stalk their ex-wife's new flame?

I flung my hands up in surrender. "Happy?"

"So, you're going tonight?" Josh asked. "A lot of people involved in the foundation will be there. It's a good place to gather suspects."

"I happen to be a fan of Rylan Blaze," I said, half-expecting my nose to grow a little.

"I couldn't get tickets." Josh fossicked in his vest until he found a handkerchief and dabbed at his brow. I was surprised a robotic arm hadn't shot out of his backpack and wiped it for him.

"I'll see what I can do," I said.

"Really?"

"No, Josh. I'm not on a case, I'm just a big fan fan of"—I channeled my inner Uncle Andy through gritted teeth—"*magic*."

Josh snorted. "You can't believe in magic. Goes against the very ethics of the Golden Age mystery thing, doesn't it? Them rules you harp on about." He counted on his fingers. "Nothing supernatural. Identical twins aren't allowed. And no magic."

He was right. "I don't believe magic is real. But I believe magicians are talented at illusion. That's all murderers are: illusionists. If you want to get away with murder, you've got two choices. You can make it look like you didn't do it, or you can make it look like someone else did. That's all a magic trick is."

"So Rylan Blaze is your suspect? If you think all magicians are killers."

"I think all killers are magicians. Not the other way around."
I thought about how that might sound in print. "You can't write
that. All of this, by the way, is off the record."

"You have to say that before we start." Josh smirked.

I noticed the little red light blinking on his shoulder camera.
"Do I?"

"How should I know? Off, on." He shrugged. "It's not like
there's a switch. People see movies and think you just say 'off
the record' and that's that. If I hear something interesting, you're
damn sure I'm printing it."

I couldn't believe I was about to try to appeal to his inner de-
cency, but it was all I had. "Just give her a chance. I'll give you an
exclusive, after."

"After what?"

"After I find the killer."

"So, you *are* investigating!" He gave me a churlish wink. "*Off* the
record, of course. And"—his cheeks glowed red with excitement—
"you think she's innocent." His eyes widened. "What *did* she tell
you to get you on side? Bet she forgot to mention she's been having
nightmares, did she? Sleepwalking? Her therapist said it's PTSD
from the mountain. Maybe she snap—"

"Her therapist is not a very good therapist if they told you this
about one of their patients." Truthfully, I only said this because I
hadn't, in fact, known about the sleepwalking and it scared me a
little. Erin had mentioned that she couldn't shake the memory of
the corpses on the mountain two and a half years ago. Psychologi-
cally, just how far can someone stretch before they break? It was
not a conversation I wanted to have with a tabloid journalist, of
all people.

"Well, her therapist has a little girl who wanted Taylor Swift
tickets—"

"I don't think nightmares and sleepwalking are enough to commit, well, *this*," I said, but Josh could hear the hesitation in my voice.

He licked the corner of his mouth, the flicker of a predator's tongue. "Things weren't rosy at home either," he said. "Lyle didn't feel safe. He called in to report a homicide yesterday."

This caught my attention. Josh knew it too. He greedily drank in my confusion.

"Yesterday?" I asked. "Who died?"

Felman shook his head. "No one. Pearse called to report an *imminent* homicide."

I thought I'd misheard. "Imminent?"

"Exactly. Weird, right?" Josh shrugged. "He caught the answering machine, which meant he didn't want to leave too much recorded, just that he was scared there was going to be a murder. And it's Christmas, the police are short-staffed, so calling him back would have been on someone's to-do list but it's hard to scream bloody murder when you don't have a victim. Cops don't act on premonitions." He sniffed. "Maybe Theresa spooked him, she's good at all that heebie-jeebie stuff." Before I could ask him who Theresa was, he rambled on. "Psychic or not, you tell me that's not a man scared of what's waiting for him at home."

"Are you telling me"—my head was spinning—"Lyle called in his *own* murder, the day before he died?"

5

REPORT YOUR OWN MURDER

CHAPTER 6

Josh put his hands on his hips, pleased to have surprised me. "*That's* a story!"

I studied him. "You sell papers if I solve crimes. Right? But the more scandalous the story, the better the sell. At first I thought it was strange you'd be so candid with me. But I figure you're choosing to tell me things that will build your best narrative. It's a better story if I try to put my ex-wife away rather than set her free. How can I trust you're giving me the whole story, not just the details—the sleepwalking, Lyle's phone call—that make Erin look guilty?"

"Believe what you want," Josh huffed. "You're not wrong about selling—though it's clicks these days, not papers, keep up—but you *are* wrong about *what* sells. This story's got legs whether you solve it or not, no matter whose side you take. I knew those facts would pique your interest, so I told you." He held up his hands. "My manipulation stops there."

"If you know all the clues, why not solve it yourself?"

Josh flashed a dark smile. "There're two stories here, mate. One, if you solve the thing. And two, if you die trying." He rubbed his fingers together in the universal sign for cash. "Hey, at least I'm honest."

It surprised me to feel a glimmer of respect at his candor. Whatever his motivation was, he'd shown no reason to sell me lies, and so his information was worth mining. "Who told you about Lyle reporting a murder? No. Wait. I assume one of the officers is a Coldplay guy."

"*The Book of Mormon*, actually."

"This is unethical journalism at its finest."

"Thank you."

"I didn't mean it as a comp—"

"So, you *don't* want the photos then?" Smugness doesn't bother creeping across Felman's face, it sprints. At that moment, it broke a world record. "People are easy, Ernest. They all want something. All I need to do is figure out what that is and give it to them. You want the photos, the photographer wants a flash holiday, my guy wants . . . well, I don't need to tell you what my airline buddy wants."

I folded my arms. "You've had your end. I talked. Now show me the photos."

He explored his pockets until he found one with a phone—it took a couple of goes, and produced a protein bar, a used tissue, and an EpiPen, on the way—then tapped away at it. I felt my own phone buzz in my pocket. I didn't even bother asking how he'd got my email: assumedly a guy at Google wanted a dinner reservation somewhere exclusive.

"Thanks," I said insincerely, and got in the car.

"Wait." Felman tapped on the window, voice muffled. I buzzed it down an inch. "I haven't even told you the real angle yet."

I sighed. "Dazzle me."

"It's about *you*."

"Rest assured. For once"—I hovered my finger on the window button—"it's *not* about me."

"You're not listening. What is this, your third mystery to solve?"

I shrugged. Technically it's a Holiday Special, which makes it two and a half, but I didn't want to get into semantics. "Your point?"

"You're a series detective now. You have a canon. Which

means"—he spun his fingers in the air—"you're due a nemesis."

"A nemesis?" I chewed the word.

"Every great detective has one. Your equal in wit, skill and mind. Which, for you, well . . . that's not the point. Do you see? Moriarty. Mr. X."

Arguably, Moriarty as Holmes's foil is overstated by modern adaptations. And Mr. X, too, was only in the final Poirot novel. In the written works, these villains are one-offs, not the stuff of ongoing pursuit. But their legacy is not in the cat-and-mouse, it's in what they take from the heroes. Holmes compromises his rationality, and Poirot, to put it simply, switches sides. A nemesis isn't about matching wits or being equal. It's about making the detective *less*.

Will I be different by the end of this telling? Well, I'll have been shot in the chest. If that counts.

Felman's beady little eyes were waiting for my agreement. I wasn't going to give him the satisfaction. "You've done your reading," I said. "But that's ridiculous."

"*Think about it!* Now you're famous, might someone use a murder to lure you in? To get you on the case. To *test* you."

"The only person who follows me around is you." I put up the window.

"I'm on your side!" Felman persisted, his knuckles leaving moist smudges on the glass as he tapped. "I want you to solve this." His pleading felt, once again, truthful. "Seriously, think about it. What if it's not about Lyle? What if it's about Erin?"

I turned the radio on to drown him out and mouthed animatedly through the glass: *I have a show to get to.*

The footage of what happened next will surely be used in the eventual documentary. I'd accidentally jammed Felman's overhanging microphone in the door when I closed the window. The whole contraption pulled him from his feet and dragged him beside the car. Luckily, the arm was sturdy enough to hold him off the ground, preventing a gravel exfoliation. I didn't see any of this—I'd watch it later on the footage from his shoulder—and only realized when I heard the *thunk* of his body on the door, at which point I slammed on the brakes, dropped the window, which released the microphone (and Felman), and hurried out of the car to help him up.

"I'm so sorry," I blathered. I didn't like the guy but I sure as hell didn't want to run him over. "I didn't notice."

"Wow," he said, then just repeated it over and over. "Wow. Just . . . *wow*."

I wondered if he was in shock. Then he looked directly at me.

"Ernest Cunningham . . ." he said, slowly enough that it seemed like he was only just remembering who I was. A concussion? His eyes seemed a little dim. Just as I was about to shepherd him into the car so that I could take him to a hospital, a huge grin smeared itself across his face. "Ernest Cunningham . . . *lashes out*!" He turned abruptly and walked away, dictating to himself: "Here I am, minding my own business, when the Slapdash Sleuth himself, Ernest Cunningham, attacks your intrepid reporter. Violence is clearly in this family's blood."

I got back in the car. I checked my phone and saw an email from Felman with JPEG attachments. He'd lived up to his end of the bargain, but my hands were shaking too badly to open them. I hadn't known his microphone was trapped in the door. Had I?

Violence is clearly in this family's blood.

Can our bodies commit acts that our minds hide from our own consciousnesses? Did the trauma of all the murders I've seen lay violence in me, like maggots in fruit? And if I had it in me, did Erin?

I surprised myself by shouting a long, frustrated note: If I wrote it out as dialogue, it would have all the vowels. It felt good to let it out. Across the parking lot, Felman staggered, winced, and rubbed his temple. I reminded myself to force him to get a concussion check when I next saw him.

I spun his theory in my head. I found it unsatisfying. One feature of an archenemy is that they aren't driven by motive. Their *want*, as Felman would put it, is the single pursuit of the detective, and the collateral bodies are merely breadcrumbs, which makes the mysteries arguably unsolvable. A murder mystery where the killer doesn't have a motive—well, that wouldn't work very well, would it?

As hard as I tried, I couldn't discount everything Felman had said. His reasoning was sound even if his deduction wasn't. While it was preposterous that this might all be about *me*, it didn't mean it had to be about Pearse.

What if someone didn't necessarily want Lyle dead, they just wanted it to look like Erin killed him?

WINCE

To:

FELICITY HERRINGTON

From:

KRIS KRINGLE

CHAPTER 7

I checked for any more journalist-barnacles before heading out of the parking lot and onto the main street toward the theater. The boundaries of the town itself wound around the edges of the plateau. The most prominent drops occurred at a place called Echo Point, where tourists crowded the lookouts, above the valley, four or five deep against the temporarily tinsel-twined railing. Three long fingers of shadow sliced across the treetops hundreds of meters below, cast by the Three Sisters, the jagged outcrop more like the spine of a stegosaurus than siblings. On the opposite side of the valley, a waterfall, seemingly impossibly, poured *up*, so strong was the wind that picked up its flow from the precipice and tossed it back onto the clifftop. An upside-down waterfall, pouring into the sky. It looked like, of all things, a magic trick.

The Pearse Theater was a remarkable curved-glass hemisphere that had the appearance of a half-buried seashell. Artistically rusted orange steel beams held the entrance maw open. Infamously, Katoomba got electric lighting four days before metropolitan Sydney and, perhaps as punishment, everything else four decades after. The hotels have pillared entranceways up long driveways, opening to grand staircases and glittering chandeliers, the guesthouses have peeling wallpaper and tearooms, and the cast-iron lampposts that line the parks look plucked straight from *The Exorcist*. The Pearse's twisting, glass behemoth stood out like a spaceship that had just landed.

I pulled up with half an hour to spare. People in black ties and satin dresses that looked like liquid milled around the foyer, beer bottles sweating in their hands. The entranceway's high glass awning was scattered in gum leaves, which filtered the light across the ground in a ripple.

Along the ceiling-high front windows hung huge banners featuring Rylan Blaze. I'd seen him on the website when I'd booked the ticket, but the ten-foot-tall version was something else. He had platinum blond hair with black roots, and an expertly shaved thin line of a beard that both accentuated his jawline and looked like a trail of ants. He wore a sparkling purple waistcoat over a white shirt that lacked buttons and subtlety, open to a hairless chest with just a hint of digitally crafted muscle. The whole ensemble was complemented by jet-black mascara and a bright white smile that seemed suspiciously to contain someone else's teeth. In one hand he held a rabbit, wearing a goofy, cartoonish stunned expression. His other hand was open to a lightning bolt descending from the top of the banner. Under his feet (gleamingly polished black leather shoes, no socks) his name was licked with fire. The subtitle proclaimed: *Prepare to Believe*. Under that, in an assumedly contractually negotiated half font size smaller: *Presented in association with Enigma Entertainment*. Another size down: *This Christmas, give generously to the Pearse Foundation. Passion creates change.*

To be honest, Rylan Blaze wasn't much of a suspect, but he was my only idea of where to start. Those rehabilitating with Lyle's foundation worked in theaters he'd built himself. His method was to buy up swathes of land in rural areas and throw up complexes that made even professional theaters in Melbourne or Sydney look like school-hall productions. The pièce de résistance every year was an annual national tour, supported and staffed by Pearse Foundation success stories, taking in eight locations over three and a half weeks and culminating in the black-tie Christmas finale at the theater here in Katoomba, where it all began. Lyle shelled out for high-profile acts. Last year's show was a comedian who would go on to be canceled for saying insensitive things online, but would wind up getting more famous by saying even more insensitive things online about how they couldn't say insensitive things online anymore.

The point is, a celebrity is hardly likely to have murdered their benefactor. Even if a crime in which a suspect is covered unknowingly in blood, while sleeping through a murder, seemed like a feat best suited to a magician. Unlikely suspects aside, I figured the show was as good a place as any to sniff around the Pearse Foundation and perhaps bump into a few people who *did* know Lyle.

"Ernest!"

I was surprised to hear my name called out above the crowd. It was hard to locate the voice with all the echoing glass, but eventually I saw a blond, chopstick-skewered bun scything above the heads in the crowd like a shark's fin. In *Jaws,* the only reason they don't show the full monster more often is because the production was plagued by faults in the mechanical shark. Spielberg had to shoot around the goofs and, in doing so, defined a whole era of cinematic suspense. I was reminded of that here, catching a flash of the approaching woman between shoulder blades and tuxedo-backs: purple lipstick, one green-shadowed eye, alternating red/green painted fingernails wrapped around a half-full champagne flute. By the time she got to me I'd re-created a Picasso-esque expectation of a colorful woman that didn't fit at all with the reality. She was primly dressed in an all black, expensively tailored suit, and stood with a military-straight back. On closer inspection, all the flashes of Christmas color in her getup were reluctantly applied, a contractual bare minimum of festivity. She stuck a right-angled hand out with a speed and rigidity that felt like I'd just bought it from a vending machine. "Was wondering when you'd get here. Flick."

It took me a second to realize it was her name rather than an instruction. "Ernest," I said, and shook her hand. "But you know that?"

"Of course. I've read your books. A dead body in town, your ex-wife a suspect, I figured it was only a matter of time until you showed up to poke around. Glad to have you here. The police will trawl through every corner of this place at a snail's pace, even if it's not relevant. Cops are like roadworks, right? The longer it takes the more they get paid. At least with you here we might get this wrapped up by Christmas. We don't need any further reputational damage." She seemed to take a second to remind her face to be solemn. I could almost hear the clanking as her internal mechanics winched her cheeks into a frown. "It's all a very sad business, obviously. Lyle was . . . well . . . he meant a lot of things to a lot of people here. How's Erin holding up?"

"She's accused of murder, about how you'd think."

"Yes. Well." She brushed the front of her jacket. "I liked her."

"You were close?"

"Not at all. Which is probably why I liked her. People are generally less likeable the more you get to know them. I certainly am." She sipped her drink. "I can look forward to disliking you, I'm sure."

"Did you like Lyle?"

She smiled. "I knew him well."

"And your role in the foundation?"

"CFO." She paused, as if only just remembering Lyle had died, then added, "Interim head now, I suppose. Felicity Herrington, if you want to be formal about it. Come on, let me show you around."

I hesitated. My snooping wasn't usually welcomed. I felt like a vampire lingering on a stoop, invited, yet peering nervously inside for hidden garlic crosses. "You say you've read my books?" Flick gave me a *time is money* eyebrow raise and nodded. "But you also say you don't want any more reputational damage."

"Your point?"

"I specialize in reputational damage." She didn't laugh. "And, just to be honest, I don't have any official qual—"

She tilted her palm and placed the edge of it first on my left shoulder, then my right, as if it were a ceremonial sword. "Deputized. Or whatever. I'd rather you sniffing about than the police. That way you can tell me what you find. Law enforcement tend to be more secretive. Deal?" She winked. "But I'm sure you won't find much. Pretty clean here. Then again, I would have said the same about Erin. Like, wow. You were married to her, right?" I nodded. She had a thick Irish accent that was taking me a few minutes to jump into the skipping rope of. "No offense, but it's not like she has"—she looked me up and down—"the killer instinct."

No offense, of course, always means *some*. I wasn't sure which part I was supposed to be partially offended by. If she was calling me dull because Erin had married me, surely that made me more exciting by virtue of our divorce.

Flick put a hand on my back, right between the shoulders, in the overfamiliar way of publicists or criminals about to execute a snitch, and guided me around the circumference of the crowd to a side door, which led away from the glass atrium to the building's interior. Swiping a keycard, she opened the door.

I followed her through but nodded behind me. "There's money

in that foyer." We passed several red-painted doors labeled with ascending numbers and the words *Dressing Room*. "Black-tie gala, Bollinger in the glasses. Blaze wouldn't come cheap either."

"Why do you think I'm stuffed into a McQueen? This isn't some lo-fi am-dram ad-hoc fundie," she said.

"I know it's corporate speak, but are there any words you don't abbreviate?"

She flicked me a wry smile over her shoulder. "N."

To my left was the dark blue light of backstage, and a black curtain. A laminated sign on the doorway said: *Stage Entrance— Quiet Please*. The wall beside us was white-painted brick, and had been signed by every performer who played the theater over the years, indecipherable squiggles of history. At the end of the hall was a staircase leading up.

Flick took the steps three at a time. There was a fresh, sweet smell in the air: like disinfectant. "That's the point, isn't it? Lyle's philo was that he didn't want people to donate out of pity, he wanted to sell them something they actually wanted. This theater was designed by Aleksander Mortgart, I assume you know his work?"

I didn't, but wasn't brave enough to say so.

"These small towns, ever since more people started working from home they've been flooded with the rich—investment bankers, tech bros."

I agreed. Regional areas were becoming towns of two halves: mansions on one side of the street and fibro on the other. Mortgart versus Shack-chic. I don't want to misrepresent regional Australia. The reason organizations like the Pearse Foundation existed here was not because any area was more susceptible to drugs or crime, but because the class divide was growing with the influx of tree-changers, and those struggling were being left behind by the gentrification. Ironically, it was the money in this very room that was causing much of that divide in the first place.

"Lyle wanted their money even without the pressure of charity," Flick continued. "So putting on a show gives them something tangible. And behold, turns out they donate and pay double anyway."

The top of the stairs opened up into a simple communal space with the opposite vibe to what Flick had just described. A semicircle of secondhand couches surrounded a television, next to a table with mismatched chairs, and off to the side was a kitchenette economically stocked with appliances pulling double duty—a toaster-microwave, a kettle-frother, and no doubt a cutlery drawer full of only sporks. The walls were painted lime green, which I thought was a bit on the nose for a green room and a choice likely not made by internationally renowned architect Aleksander Mortgart.

The television was on, broadcasting live video of the stage and the front few rows of seats. The picture was grainy but color. The audience hadn't been let in yet, but people were variously wandering across the stage. A man was pointing up at the ceiling, clearly checking the lighting. A young woman dressed as a reindeer ran a cloth over a large wooden guillotine prop before another person with their back to the camera wheeled it offstage.

Yes, I'm aware that someone with their back to a security camera is an instant suspect. It's like wrapping a Toblerone for Christmas. What's the point? How many other triangular-prism shaped objects am I likely to receive?

In the corner of the green room stood a real pine tree, trussed in silver tinsel and gently pulsing lights. That was the scent I'd noticed on the stairs. Whether pine needles actually smell like disinfectant, or we have simply made disinfectant smell like pine needles for so long the association is ubiquitous, I'm still not sure. Underneath the tree was a small collection of presents, five in total. The largest was a square box wrapped in blue cellophane, a tag scribbled directly onto the wrapping in black Texta: *To: Rylan Blaze, From: KK.*

I heard a patter of feet up the stairs behind me, and a short pale girl burst into the room. She was wearing theater blacks: t-shirt, pants and work boots. It's an outfit designed not to be seen. Without speaking, Flick held out a hand. The girl pulled a fist-sized present from a tote bag she had slung over her shoulder, and handed it to Flick like a sacred object.

Flick snatched it, shook it next to her ear. "Who'd I get again?"

"Theresa," squeaked the assistant.

"I trust you know your sister well enough to have picked something good," Flick said, then turned to me. "Our warm-up act. A hypnotist. Though I'm sure you don't believe in such things." Back to her assistant. "Remind me the price limit?"

"Twenty dollars."

Flick weighed the little box in her hand. "This cost twenty?"

"Yes, ma'am."

"Not nineteen? Eighteen-fifty?"

The girl fidgeted with the cuff of her sleeve. "Maybe nineteen."

"Receipt and change please, Sam."

"I . . . ah . . ." Sam fumbled the words. "I got it wrapped, which was a gold coin donation." She winced, and added quickly, "It was for a good cause."

"Do I look like a charity to you?"

"You do, actually," I added, trying to defuse the tension. "Quite literally."

Flick snorted a derisive laugh, then handed the box back to Sam, who walked over and placed the present on top of the blue box addressed to Rylan before scurrying off downstairs.

"Don't want to get the boss," I said, pointing to the presents. "That's the problem with Secret Santa. Look at the size of that box. Whoever got Rylan felt the pressure to make it good; they spent more than twenty."

"That's why Lyle always rigs it so he gets me. So he doesn't have to play favorites." Flick's brow furrowed. "*Didn't* play favorites, I suppose. That'll take some getting used to." She stilled. I thought I saw a glimmer of sadness, though perhaps it was merely analytical impatience at the inconvenience of having to rejig her grammar.

"So you're profitable, then?" I said. "Building multi-million-dollar complexes in small towns isn't exactly a tinned food drive. After you fund the rehabilitation programs, what's left over?"

Flick led me across the room to a locked office door, *Lyle Pearse* slotted into an aluminum label holder. "We have a turnover that reflects the investment, and before you ask, yes, our staff," she gestured to herself, "are compensated. The key to a good business is to run it like a charity. People will spend more if they believe it's ethical. The key to running a good charity"—she wagged a finger—"is to run it like a business."

Conceptually, I understood her point. But emotionally, all I could think was: If a charity was a business, what did that make the people Flick was helping? Products?

"How much money would you lose if you canceled tonight?"

"The man who cashes in on murders thinks it's in poor taste to run the show?" She chuckled. "This is *for* Lyle. It's his legacy. If you died tomorrow, you'd want someone to publish your notes, no?" That was fair. I opened my mouth to apologize, but Flick wasn't finished. "Before you think I've gone soft: sad hearts equal open wallets."

"Thinking like that must require, how did you say it before, a killer instinct?" I said.

"I'm as cutthroat as they come, but I didn't kill Lyle." She got the keycard out again, swiped it on Lyle's office door and then handed it to me. "Here you go. Full access."

"Did you know you'd be promoted to acting head if—"

"Interim head."

"Interim head," I repeated. It occurs to me now that such a title would be better suited to another person in the events to come, but of course I didn't know that at the time. "But the foundation had a succession plan in case something like this happened, right? That seems a sensible part of a business strategy. You would have known you were in line."

"Yes, I suppose I did." She stepped into Pearse's office. "But this isn't *Hamlet*. It's a magic show."

To:
SAM LIN

From:
GUESS WHO (hehe)

CHAPTER 8

Pearse's office contained one very significant clue, and the omission of another.

At first glance, though, the meaning of both what was and what wasn't there went over my head. The office looked entirely unremarkable: a desktop computer, an electric-powered standing desk with an adjustable height, and a leather office chair with a high back and headrest, on which was strapped a robotic neck massager. Two egg-shaped chairs were in front of the desk. Unlike the green room, this office had brand-new furniture. Above the door perched a television, which was switched on to the same channel broadcasting the live stage stream as the screen outside.

The walls were ringed with framed photographs of Lyle shaking hands with various politicians and celebrities. He'd been dating Erin about two years, and looked the same even in old photos as he had the few times I'd met him. He was a top-heavy, wide-shouldered man with a penchant for skinny jeans, so he looked a little cartoonish, his waist to his shoulders forming a large V. He was always clean-shaven with slick silver hair. When I'd first heard about Erin's new squeeze, I'd felt that guilty yet human validation that he was much older than I was, until I'd met him and found him in far superior shape. I'd say he was the definition of ageing gracefully, if he wasn't already dead.

I'd meant what I'd tried to say to Erin back in the police station. I found Lyle to be a generous man: pistols-at-dawn-quick with his wallet around a drinks bill. At the time, I assumed this generosity was characteristic of someone who ran a rehab charity. Of course, I hadn't met Flick yet. I did believe Lyle had been good for Erin. *Too good*, she'd whispered to me once, early on in their dating. *Sometimes I feel like a project.* I thought they'd go the distance. 'Til death do us . . . well, even unmarried they'd fulfilled any prospective vows better than Erin and I had, I suppose.

I spotted a photo taken in the familiar gleaming glass atrium, a large crowd gathered around a red ribbon, a journalist, back to the camera, arms open in a frozen attempt to scooch the crowd together for the shot. Pearse brandished a gigantic set of ornamental bronze scissors. The little plaque said: *Opening of the Pearse Foundation Inaugural Theater, 2019.*

Obviously photographs in mystery novels are important. I'll be honest and tell you that, of course, there is a murderer in this image. So let's unpack it.

I didn't know everyone's faces, but I could see Flick, seemingly annoyed to be asked to take a second to smile, surprisingly with bright blue hair. Sam, a sullen teenager, stood behind her. Actually, it looked like there were two Sams. A young girl in a floral dress stood closer to the front of the group: she had Sam's face. To the groans of mystery readers everywhere, it looks like we have *twins* on our hands.

Now, let me clarify. Twins are only unfair in a mystery if they aren't introduced honestly to the reader. That's to protect from the dreaded *switch* twist. And I've been upfront here that these two are identical. So even though they do both switch, in a way, later on, it's all still fair play.

Flick saw me take a photo with my phone and smiled. "We opened on the ten-year anniversary of the foundation. You want to know if the whole hamster wheel works? This is Christopher." She smudged a fingerprint on the glass at a man in his late twenties, applauding, red-cheeked with joy. "He came to us when he was fifteen, and by this time he was at university for a psychology degree. Now he's our head counselor. One of our first success stories. And Dinesh," she said, with another smudge on a brown-skinned man with a long black ponytail and glasses. "Twenty seventeen, I think? Struggled for a while, has a short fuse, dropped in and out of the rehab camps, but once we opened the theater, well, it was like he was at home. He's grown into our production manager, and even though he's above the pay grade, still likes to get his hands dirty and op the LX for Blaze." She gave me an exasperated look. "*Operate* the *lights*."

"I'm surprised to see you've got a rebellious streak." I pointed. At her confusion I added, "Blue hair?"

Her nostrils flared. "Prank by the kids. Swapped my shampoo bottle. Lyle was bloody in on it too. Said it was good for morale. Told me to loosen up."

"You strike me as someone who responds well to that." I didn't bother hiding the sarcasm.

"Some detective." She remained unimpressed. "Honestly, though, looking back on it, I get it. The kids deserve a laugh."

"How'd the twins find you? Sam and . . . Theresa, right? She's the hypnotist in the show?"

Much to my satisfaction, she stopped smudging the glass and instead tapped a fingernail on the girl in the floral dress. "Theresa flew through, one of our most responsive to the program, I'd hazard. Which is especially rare in a seventeen-year-old, as she is here. She's just graduated, if I remember correctly. Sam's, well, she's a good kid, but has had a few more challenges. In and out, addiction can be a yo-yo. She's been doing well the last year. I think the structure of us working together has really helped her."

On closer inspection of the photo, there was a difference in energy between the twins. Theresa practically glowed with enthusiasm, while Sam hid farther back, trying to disappear in the crowd.

"Oh, and this is Shaun Martin, a young-un then too." Flick pointed at a shiny-cheeked youth in a t-shirt and cargo shorts; as I will eventually learn, the guy with his back to the live-stream camera from before. "Like Sam, when we took this photo he was still in the program. Turned it around with a love of, of all things, magic. Went viral on YouTube and TikTok with his tricks. Rylan Blaze hired him a year or so ago as his prop master, so it's good to have him back here for a few weeks. It's how Lyle got the idea to approach Blaze for this year's tour." Flick sighed, like her memory was a warm bath. "Just looking at this shows me all the lives we've saved." She snapped out of it and whipped her attention back to me. "Well, aside from Lyle's, obviously."

I stepped back from the photo and took in the rest of the office. The walls were surprisingly bare: no framed degrees or certificates of education, though there was a hole in the plaster, too far off the ground to be made by a fist. A bookshelf was absent of spines, but filled with entrepreneurial and acting awards, including a polished heavy metallic pyramid that sat askew, as if hastily replaced, and, in any mystery other than this one, would end up a murder weapon. Another trophy was an exact glass replica of an Academy Award, with a silver plaque attached that read *It Was Worth It*. Lyle's acting wasn't exactly Oscar-winning material, in my opinion, so it seemed a little arrogant, but it was a finely crafted replica. The middle shelf held a cheap supermarket chocolate advent calendar: a flimsy cardboard box with twenty-four rubbery, oversweet chocolates behind each perforated door, one for each day of December leading up to and finishing on Christmas Eve. I explain this only because my stepsister Sofia, who is from Ecuador, had mentioned one Christmas lunch that she'd never had an advent calendar and didn't even know what it was. My uncle Andy decided to rectify what he called "a vicious crime against culture" and bought one for her the next year. Of course, because it was Andy, it wasn't any normal advent calendar: every five days or so the door opened on no chocolate and the words *Life's Not Fair*.

This advent calendar had four unopened doors. For the first time I was really hit by the gravity of Lyle's death: I'd been so focused on the puzzle I hadn't considered what he'd left behind. The advent calendar felt like a horrible metaphor: unopened doors left over from an unfinished life.

Then I realized something.

"He's opened the wrong doors," I said.

"Huh?" Flick said. She was standing by the doorway waiting for me to finish up, tapping on her phone. "Oh, that bloody thing. Lyle loved those, had one every year."

"Today's the twenty-first, right?" I fiddled with the little paper door, levering it back and forth. "He's opened it. Erin told me they went to sleep at half past eleven, and Lyle was dead when she woke up in the morning." I thought a second. Erin had gotten up to use the bathroom, at my approximation, at around or just after one a.m. *I don't know*, she'd said, when I asked if she noticed Lyle in their enormous bed. *I wish I did*. I'd asked her this to ascertain whether he might have been dead in the kitchen downstairs at the time, but perhaps he wasn't in the house at all. "So he came into the theater in the middle of the night." I spun it out slowly. "Unless he opened two yesterday. Greedy."

Flick shook her head. "*It's about self-control*," she said, deepening her voice and puffing out her chest. Even with the little time I'd spent with Lyle, it was a clear but bad imitation. "He was all about consistency. *You could have it all at once if you wanted, but then you'd have nothing left for tomorrow.*"

"He's not that consistent," I said, studying the advent calendar. "There's still the right number of doors *open*. He's missed the twelfth. Was he on the road?"

"Blaze was at"—Flick counted off imaginary dates on her fingers—"Toowoomba." That was nearly a thousand kilometers north. "Lyle doesn't travel with the tour. That's me and Sam, Theresa with her opening act, and Shaun."

"And Dinesh?" I offered.

"Not Toowoomba, no."

"You said he did the lights?"

"He had a—" She swallowed and, believe me, it was as suspicious then as it is writing it out here. "Family emergency. Dropped out of the second half of the tour."

I could tell that was as much juice as she'd squeeze, so I turned my attention to Lyle's desk. His computer setup was unique: the keyboard was pushed to the back, basically out of reach, and instead an upright trapezoidal microphone stood in front of the monitor.

"*Dictation saves you up to point four seconds per minute, which is equivalent to two million dollars in a lifetime,*" Flick said from behind me. "Lyle loved those bloody entrepreneurial audiobooks. I don't get it, myself."

I wriggled the mouse and the computer flashed to life, but there was nowhere to type the password.

"Voice password," Flick said, and then anticipated my next question with an eye roll. "No idea."

I leaned into the microphone and put on a version of Flick's deep-throated mimicry. "Pearse."

The screen shuddered in denial. One of the rules of murder mysteries is that the detective cannot succeed by virtue of luck or coincidence. My amateur hacking doesn't cut the mustard. There is, of course, a password to Pearse's computer. I've actually already seen it somewhere. But I'm going to have to earn it.

I settled on old school and rifled through the drawers, finding a paper diary. When I picked it up, a ripped page from another notebook fluttered out: a schematic of some kind, roughly sketched in pencil. It appeared to be a gun with dotted lines representing bullet trajectories toward a bull's-eye. Only the dashed lines didn't make it the whole way to the target: they stopped in the middle, halted by another vertical line. Below the gun were several three-dimensional sketches of two bullets, one with a W on the circular bottom; the other was blank. Flick was distracted by her phone. I wasn't sure she'd even seen the paper fall out of the diary, so I put the schematic in my pocket.

I turned the diary to December 12. An empty page stared back. "Nothing in here, out of town or otherwise, on the twelfth."

"So he missed a day," Flick said. "I don't know what to tell you. I don't supervise the chocolate consumption. Who cares?"

"That I don't know yet." I looked around the desk. It was sterile, too clean, not a mug or a dish, not even a single pen. Minimalism is endemic among entrepreneurs: Society should be paper*less*, or cash*less*, cars should be driver*less*. Put this VR headset on and be life*less*. Flicking through, it seemed Lyle barely used the physical diary, which likely meant the fact that it was empty was meaningless. I needed to get into the computer.

A wiry man popped his head around the door. While he was thin enough that I noticed he'd pierced his own holes into his watchband to go around his matchstick wrists, he didn't seem slight. Rather he had the wound-up tightness of a marathon runner. I recognized him easily, even with five extra years and less hair on him than the photograph.

"Fifteen-minute call, Flick," he said. Noticing me, he said, "Oh, hi," and extended his hand. He had shiny spots on his fingers, likely thermal burns from his drug use as a youth. "Christopher Sleet." He spoke with a slight lisp and had thinning brown hair that was front-loaded, a wisp of which I would come to learn he had a habit of blowing up out of his eyes between sentences. He wore a crumpled bow tie he'd lost a battle with (that's *all* bow ties, for those who've ever tried to tie one). He returned his attention to Flick. "Hiring detectives, are we?"

"Happenstance hires me," I said.

"Solve it, and I'm sure we can find you a payment better than that." Flick looked between me and Christopher. "If you recognize Ernest, I'll skip the introductions. I was just showing him around. I figured the police would be indelicate."

"I've been hearing your praises sung, Christopher," I said. He waved off the compliment, a move he clearly repeated often. "I understand Pearse had such an impact on your life you wanted to give the same back to others?"

"Yes, but"—he dodged the compliment again—"I didn't make some big sacrifice like Lyle did coming back here at the peak of his career. I studied art a little first in Sydney, but I couldn't quite get the hang of it. So I rejigged my degree."

"The hang of it?" Flick scoffed. "You're underselling yourself."

"Do you think Lyle ever regretted his decision?" I asked.

Christopher considered this. "The honest answer is: I hope not. I mean that. I think there are enough reminders in this place, in the people"—while he was speaking, Flick plucked the bootleg Academy Award off the shelf and held it up like a showgirl on a gameshow—"and some more unsubtle messaging, if it makes you happy, Flick." He laughed, then looked back at me. "I gave

Lyle that. I know. *It Was Worth It*." He wrinkled his nose. "It is a bit cheesy."

"I don't quite see the meaning," I confessed.

"I wanted to give him an 'Oscar,' show him that what he'd done here was more valuable than what he might have done over in Hollywood. I thought maybe he could look at it and feel he hadn't traded a better life for this one."

"Do you feel you traded art?"

"Not for a second. Like I said, it really wasn't a big deal."

I got the feeling not much was a big deal for Christopher. He possessed a calm, relaxing tone. I wanted to put my feet up on a couch and tell him my problems.

"He had a scholarship," Flick said to me, with a tone like she was dobbing at school. "A calling's a calling. This is a good reminder to more than just Lyle," she said, turning the trophy in her hand. I wondered if she was talking to Christopher or herself. Did she have something she'd traded for this?

I decided to make the most of Christopher's presence; he would know the foundation's current and past intake a little more personally than Flick. "So, as for the current graduates and participants, how far through the program is everyone who's working on the Blaze tour?"

"Well, obviously there's a whole crew that's not in the foundation. But"—Christopher counted it out on his fingers—"Sam's graduated twice, although right now is back in. She's on track though, we're all proud of her. Theresa finished about when this theater opened. While it's upsetting that their home life has turned them both to us, on the other hand, it's quite the endorsement that Theresa has pulled her sister up with her. Dinesh's been with us since before we opened this place, probably four years clean if I had to guess. Shaun finished about eighteen months ago, just before his videos went viral and caught Rylan's management's eye. A clever kid, hands on. Always had an interest in engineering, mechanics, all that kind of thing. We couldn't be more thrilled for him."

"Boss?" Sam poked her head in.

Flick turned to me. "You'll keep me updated, yeah?" I nodded. "You've got the key, come and go as you please. The passcode to the theater is . . ." She shot a mistrustful eye at Sam, then handed me a business card with her mobile number on it. "Prank me. I'll text it to you." She disappeared out of the room with an air of crisp dismissal. Christopher excused himself behind her, pulling a deck of palm cards from his jacket pocket and rehearsing a speech in a mutter as he headed toward the stage.

Sam lingered in the doorway. She had panda eyes and a nervous, flighty demeanor. "Four, one, eight, three," she said, after Flick had left. "The alarm. I don't know how she thinks I get in here before her every day."

"Was Lyle a good boss?" I asked.

Sam nearly choked getting her answer out. "He saved my life. More than once. I was dealing and using, no one else would have given me a job. And he did. Not only that, but when I stuffed it all up again, guess what? The door's still open. So yeah"—she ground the toe of her shoe into the carpet—"I guess."

"Flick works you pretty hard, does she?"

"It's an important job."

"You've been on the tour with your sister?"

"She's the opening act." Her eyes flicked up. "Perfect Theresa. Of course the stage loves her." She seemed momentarily ashamed of the comment. "Mr. Cunningham, I don't have time for questions. I have a show to start."

"It's Ernest. And it's only one question. You're across Flick's schedule. I wonder if you're across Lyle's? I know you were in Toowoomba. Any idea if he was here on the twelfth?"

Sam chewed her lip. It was clear she wasn't so much deciding what to tell me, but deciding what Flick *wanted* her to tell me. She appeared to decide that, given Flick had invited me in, she was supposed to answer my questions. "He's a workaholic. He's here all the time in the buildup to the big finale, including weekends. Plus he had that meeting with Dinesh. I had to charter a jet so they could get here and then Rylan could make it back in the day. Happy?" She didn't even bother waiting for my answer, just hurried off.

I lingered in the office, searching for any further clues or passwords. Flick had told me Dinesh had left the tour in Toowoomba because of a family emergency. But instead, he'd flown back here, with Rylan alongside, to meet with Lyle. And yet, according to the chocolates, Lyle might not have even set foot in his office.

On my own now, I tried to remember the way back to the front, but being deep in a theater is like being in a submarine: there's no sense of direction. I heard voices, a blue-painted door nearby slightly ajar.

"Come on, Tee," huffed a voice I recognized as Sam's. "It's not fair. Please swap."

I peered through the crack. Inside, I could see Theresa, dressed in a sparkly light brown reindeer bodysuit, fluffy cuffs on her wrists and ankles. A bright red bulbous nose overtook her face, like a fat frog on a small lily pad. She had a long, healed scar on the inside of one wrist.

"I've already bought my Secret Santa," Theresa-Rudolph said.

"But I've got—"

"Don't tell me who you've got, Sam! Geez!" Theresa whipped

open the door. I flattened myself against the wall, purely out of guilt from eavesdropping, but she had her back to me. "That's the whole point of the thing. *Honestly*."

Theresa strode off back toward the stage, Sam trotting a few steps behind. I wondered who was so difficult to buy for that Sam was desperate to hand them off. I also guessed, from tone and dominance, that Theresa was the older sister. It might have only been minutes, but older siblings are older siblings.

I'd taken a wrong turn. I backtracked until I found myself alongside the red-painted dressing rooms. As I hurried past, one of the dressing room nameplates caught my eye: *Rylan Blaze.*

I checked my phone: ten minutes to showtime. I doubted he'd be in there but thought I'd try my luck anyway, and knocked. No answer. I wriggled the door handle: locked. I turned to go, but then remembered I had the keycard Flick had given me. She had said *full access.* Did that mean all doors? I held it up, and the door lock blipped, whirred, and, to my surprise, turned green.

I opened the door, and Rylan Blaze's decapitated head rolled out into the hallway.

**DECEMBER
TWELFTH**

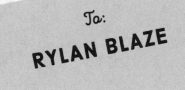

To:

RYLAN BLAZE

From:

KK

CHAPTER 9

Bloody thing keeps getting away from me!" Rylan laughed, picking up his own head. He ushered me into the dressing room and closed the door behind us.

It is, both from the magician and in these pages, a cheap cliffhanger of a trick. I apologize. But, believe me, for a flicker of a second I did leap backward in shock. It was a very good replica, but not one that held up to close scrutiny: glassy eyes and a wide-open mouth. A little bit of jagged red paint around the stump, as well as what looked like real hair. The texture was slightly glossy, fine varnish on modeling clay, clearly enough to fool an audience under stage lights, but not enough for a detective in a brightly lit corridor. Well, not for more than a second anyway.

Rylan looked up from his replica and took me in, momentarily confused. He sniffed, wiped his nose, and pulled his dressing gown a little tighter over his chest. I noticed he was clean shaven, with only his mustache and half of his black beard glued on. The room was like a tornado had hit a carnival—colorful scarves and top hats and flowers were littered all over a portable clothes rack and couch. The bench space was equally cluttered: the other half of Rylan's beard, a white dove in a small cage, two upright bullets, and even a blender were among the debris. This was all backdropped by a wall-length mirror ringed by bare lightbulbs.

Rylan put his fake head down with a *thunk* in front of the mirror. "Who are you, exactly?"

"I'm looking into things with Lyle Pearse." I nodded to Rylan's general state of undress. "Aren't you on in ten minutes?"

"They've got to get all that charity shit out of the way first." Rylan walked into the bathroom. From the sheer volume of sniffing that seeped into the room, I very much doubted he was aware of the irony of headlining a drug rehabilitation gala. "Plus the warm-up chick. Looking into Lyle, like an auditor?"

"Sure." Chalk this up to something I've learned in my training-wheel detective hours: if you agree with people they tend to keep talking.

Rylan poked his head out of the bathroom. His glued-on mustache had come unstuck and flapped as he talked. There might not be snow in this Christmas tale, given the setting, but there was a White Christmas on Rylan's top lip. "Well, you can tell Lyle that the valuation is about half a million *over*. My guys say your outgoings don't match up." He ducked back inside.

"Valuation?"

"That's the reason I'm touring these holes." I heard a tap running. "I'm scoping out the sites before my company invests."

"Lyle is looking to sell the business?"

"Aren't you an auditor?"

"You do know that Lyle is—"

"Tough as nails, yeah, I know." Rylan stepped out of the bathroom, this time in full costume, hair perfectly tousled. It was miraculous how quickly he'd turned from a man in his underpants to a fully-fledged showman, and I have to confess I felt a little starstruck. "But tell him I *walk* on nails for a living. He can stew on that."

There went my lead suspect: Rylan Blaze didn't even know Lyle was dead.

"Why do you want to invest in, as you say, *holes*?" I emphasized his word choice, making it clear I disagreed. Katoomba was a world-famous natural paradise, but I supposed it lacked the casino and strip club required to meet Rylan's personal definition of a great township.

"The theaters, man. It's like making music. What do all great musicians do to really make money? They don't play for other people, they start their own label. Pssht. Business is boring, have a drink with me." Rylan fossicked around under the bench top and pulled out a bottle of unlabeled red wine. I must have visibly hesitated because he added, "I can tell you're a connoisseur. Bargain bin, yes, I'll give you that. But good wine is all about aeration—right? Check this out." He upended the bottle over the blender, let about half of it glug in, then whacked the lid on and pressed start. While it blended he produced two wineglasses from inside his jacket pocket with a flourish. After about twenty seconds, he turned off the blender, sloshed the wine into the two glasses, and handed me one. "Mr. Auditor, bottoms up."

I wrinkled my nose at the glass. I'm not, in fact, much of a connoisseur, but I did know that having so many bubbles in a glass was at odds with good drinking. I took a ginger sip, and was rewarded with nothing more than a glass of four-dollar wine.

Rylan, however, looked pleased with himself. "Remarkable, right?"

"Remarkable," I agreed, not talking about the wine. Like a glass atrium or a glued-on mustache.

Rylan gulped down his glass. The room stank of alcohol. I suppose the wine was aerated, because it felt like I was breathing it.

"Don't you need to be sober? Aren't your stunts dangerous?" I asked.

"You mean getting out of the straitjacket before I get blown apart by a cannonball?" He snorted. "It's all tricks, mate. Besides, I'm not getting my noggin lopped off." He tossed me his head and I caught it one-handed. "It's this fella." Model-Rylan stared up at me, still surprised by his own decapitation. "The only dangerous trick is the bullet catch," Real-Rylan said. He picked up the two bullets, presenting them to me one by one. "Real bullet. Wax bullet. Pass around the real bullet to the audience, just so it looks convincing, though most punters won't know the difference anyway, then palm it off before loading the gun. The gun fires normally but the heat of the firing dissolves the wax in the air before it gets close enough to me to do any damage. Then I've just got to—" He hocked up some gunk and spat in the wineglass. A crumpled bullet tinkled into the glass bowl. "Ta da." He grinned. "Magicians aren't supposed to give away our secrets, but you and I are business partners, so you get special treatment. Can't wait to get rid of these thieving bastards and hire some professionals."

It took me a moment to work out what he meant. "Thieving? You mean the graduates of the program?"

"Lyle'll tell you about it. That's why you've got to help us close this deal quick—" He paused, held both bullets up to the light. "No. Hang on, maybe this one." He shuffled the bullets around. "Which is the wax?" He tossed them between his hands again and squinted.

A knock at the door didn't wait for a response and a sharply dressed young man in top hat and tails entered the dressing room. I recognized the grown version of the boy who Flick had named Shaun from the ribbon-cutting photograph. The one who was good with gadgets and had gone viral for his own magic tricks before being brought on as Rylan's prop master.

Shaun waved a hand and we swapped names. "Aren't you the de—" Shaun said cautiously.

I cut him off before he could blow my lie open in front of Rylan. "I'm looking into things. Flick said it was cool. Don't worry." I put a finger to my lips. "I won't tell any magicians' secrets."

"Flick *invited* you? Tonight?" Shaun's mouth flapped. "Never mind. Not to be rude, but we're in a rush." Then to Rylan: "You've got five minutes. And dove shit on your shoes."

"Shaun, which one of these is the wax bullet?" Rylan asked.

"The one in your left hand, you idiot. And follow the marks on the prop table: real one in your left pocket, wax in your right. Don't get them mixed up. Wax has a *W* on its base for emergencies. And please stop tossing your head about." Shaun took the fake head from me. "Wētā, the guys who worked on *Lord of the Rings*, made it. It's very expensive."

"Yes, Mother," Rylan said, churlish.

This explained the drawing I'd found in Lyle's office: It diagrammed how the bullet catch trick worked. The dashed line stopped halfway to the target because that was the point at which the wax dissipated. Whoever had drawn it had been measuring the safe distance to stand.

What followed next was a flurry of prop-checking, pocket-filling, wires clipped to other wires underneath Rylan's jacket, and shoe-polishing (done by Shaun, of course). At the end of it all, Shaun plucked my wineglass out of my hand, rinsed it, collapsed it into a flat plastic disc and shoved it back into Rylan's jacket, grumbling, "Stop drinking from the props."

Once this was finished, I tailed them out of the room and to the wings of the stage, where I glimpsed another table full of props. Sam and Theresa waited next to it, Theresa bouncing on her tiptoes with excitement, Sam more stoic and focused. I could hear Flick's voice echoing through the auditorium speaker, and though it was dulled by the curtain I caught words like *milestone* and *best-ever,* followed by a loud roar from the crowd.

Shaun placed the two bullets on the prop table, then brought Rylan over to him, rolled a lint roller along his arms and placed and straightened a top hat on his head. Shaun took magicians' secrets more seriously than Rylan, because it seemed like this whole routine was deliberately blocking my view of the prop table, to stop me from seeing the mechanics of any more tricks. When Shaun had finished dusting, he turned back to the prop table and ran a hand over it, I assumed ticking off each trick's components on a mental checklist. One of the bullets had fallen over, so he straightened it, after which he stepped back and examined the table, like a parent proud of a Christmas spread.

I could tell that Shaun was to Rylan what Sam was to Flick: the one who kept the gears turning.

Rylan had wandered out of the wings. He hovered by the brick wall, glancing over the signatures of past performers. As I watched, he produced a Sharpie, pulled the cap off with his teeth, and spat it on the ground.

"You can't be here." Sam popped up in front of me, distracting me from Rylan's signature attempt. She now wore a chunky pair of headphones with a microphone wrapped to her jaw and a little blue light clipped to her shoulder: it looked like she was ready to pilot a helicopter. "Performers only."

I obliged. Besides, I wanted to witness this bullet catch from the crowd. To see if I could, having been let in on the secret, spot the dissolution of the wax bullet in the air. But that's the thing about magicians, isn't it? Or mystery writers. When the trickster tells you where to look, you should be looking somewhere else.

The last thing I witnessed, before I hurried back down the hallway to take my seat for the performance, was Shaun tugging Rylan away from the wall. "It's bad luck to sign an autograph before the show," Shaun was saying.

"Seriously?" Rylan brushed Shaun off and finished his signature with a pointed theatrical flourish. "Sometimes I swear you believe all this mumbo jumbo magic stuff."

9

WAX BULLET

CHAPTER 10

Despite, or perhaps because of, my late booking, my seat was dead center of the front row. I squeezed down the aisle of plush red seats to a chorus of mutters and groans—one woman made an exaggerated point of checking her watch—as Christopher, stationed at a lectern in front of a ruby-red drape, struggled through an introductory speech that, judging by the number of times he shuffled his palm cards and wiped his brow, he had recently inherited from a dead man.

"Before I thank our key sponsors tonight, I want to touch on today's tragedy."

The squeak of 920 seats (I looked it up later) as people shifted in them echoed through the theater. I doubted Rylan was listening in the wings to the *charity shit* but, if he was, I imagined it would be quite the shock. I wondered why Shaun hadn't given him the heads up. Unless no one *wanted* him to know, I thought.

"Lyle Pearse saved my life when I was fifteen. Mine was the first of many. And, to be honest, we weren't sure if we could go through with tonight at all." Christopher paused. "But all of us here at the foundation also know that Lyle wouldn't have wanted to cancel this important night. So it might feel a little strange, but I encourage you to have fun. Enjoy yourselves. And when the time comes, dig deep. Because celebrating what Lyle has built is the best way I can think of to celebrate the man himself."

This received thunderous applause. Christopher wiped his eyes with the back of his hand, then looked back at the palm cards. I looked around the theater. The inside was as opulent as the atrium.

The seating was organized in a ring not unlike Shakespeare's Globe, with two balconies above the stalls and corporate boxes to the sides. A trio of spotlights shone from a windowed booth on the second balcony, where I glimpsed Dinesh's reflection operating the lighting desk. The stage was framed by Roman-inspired columns clasped by twisting stone nymph figures, and the ceiling was painted a navy blue with pinpricks of firefly lights. It looked like we were out under the stars in a Grecian amphitheater.

While Christopher rattled off contractually required corporate mentions, I pulled out my phone and opened the email from Josh Felman. He'd sent six crime scene images. The blood seemed bright red, ready to leap off the screen. I put a cupped hand over the phone and lowered the brightness, checking either side of me for inquisitive eyes, but most people were politely focused on Christopher's speech. While he spoke, I looked at his hero, dead on my phone.

Lyle lay on his back in a kitchen, wearing flannelette pajama bottoms, despite the heat, but bare-chested. His stomach was mush. Stabbed, as I knew, multiple times. I could see why Erin hadn't bothered with CPR. One arm was extended out from his side. His fingertip was red, and at the end of the arm, written in blood on the floor, was a single word: *Christmas*.

I blinked twice. I know this is a Holiday Special, but I was hardly expecting the victim's final word to be festive.

The next photo was a close-up of the word. The letters were smeared, clearly written with difficulty and in pain, and jumbled in size: an enormous *h* compared to a short and stumpy *t*. I imagined Lyle ink-blotting his own torso, trying to write it out before he died. Why that one word? And if he'd had time to leave a message, then why hadn't he called out to Erin, sleeping upstairs?

I shuddered at my own answer to this: imagining Lyle's lungs filling with blood.

I quickly opened the rest of the photos. The staircase, blood dripped in a path. The knife, dropped at the top of the stairs. Tousled, blood-stained bedsheets. I felt an elbow in my ribs, and a grunt of implied rudeness, and returned my attention to the stage. From my seat, I could see into the wings, where Sam was speaking rapidly into her headset.

"I am proud to lead a new generation of young people through that dark tunnel. To show them that there is a way out. And, most of all, that everyone deserves a second chance." Christopher had relaxed now that he was wrapping up. "Before we see the main event, this year's foundation partner Rylan Blaze, let me tell you about a different kind of magic trick, an old classic that transforms objects into other objects. You can take a stack of hundred-dollar bills, see here ten of them"—he reached into his jacket and withdrew a bundle of notes, held together by an elastic band— "and you can turn these thousand dollars into a bed for a week for a youth in need. You can turn ten of these into a placement on one of our rehabilitation camps. You can turn fifty of these into a new counselor for our team. Or, if you're feeling magical, you can turn a bunch of these into a theater just like this one. But I won't tell you how many that takes." He winked. "All you've got to do now is enjoy yourselves. Remember, this is a *celebration*. Clap, hoot, holler and stamp your feet. Lyle is up there somewhere." He looked up to the ceiling in reverence. "Let him hear you."

CHAPTER 11

Theresa's reindeer hypnotist act was competently unspectacular. She'd bring people up from the crowd, tap them brutishly on the forehead, make them squawk like a chicken or recite *Romeo and Juliet*, and then click her fingers and send her victims back to their seats, seemingly clueless about what they'd just done. I was skeptical if she was truly erasing their memories or if the volunteers were audience plants. Still, it was enough to distract the attention of my elbow-trigger-happy neighbor, which allowed me to return to my phone.

The final photo in Josh's email was a close-up of Lyle's outstretched arm, ending at his blood-inked fingertip. At first I wondered what the point of this additional photo was. Then I noticed something on the arm, right in the crook of the elbow. A small dot. I zoomed in. It looked like a needle mark.

I was stunned. The founder of a drug rehabilitation charity, found dead with a needle mark in his arm?

My phone buzzed. A text message blipped above the photo, from Juliette:

The Slapdash Sleuth Strikes Out?

Busted. I'd known it was only a matter of time until Josh published a story, but I'd still hoped to stay a little bit ahead of it. I was also a tad surprised that Juliette was a subscriber to his column. I flicked back a text quickly.

I can explain.

Juliette rang. Even on silent, the rattling of my phone was enough to annoy my seat neighbor, who shot me some side-eye.

I gave him an apologetic wince and texted back: I'm in the theater. Text only.

Juliette: Erin?

Me: She asked me to come.

Juliette: Give me the skinny.

Me: It's nothing, Julz, I swear. I'm not cavorting around the mountains with my ex.

Juliette: Hang on. What?

Me: We're long divorced. You don't need to worry. I shouldn't have come.

Theresa finished her routine with three volunteers doing an embarrassing disco dance, and the theater roared their approval. The clapping from the seat next to me was particularly pointed, angled more at me than the stage. As Theresa trotted off, glowing red nose bobbing, the floor-to-ceiling red drape suddenly dropped, revealing a gimmicky but nevertheless impressive set designed to look like Santa's workshop.

To a murmur of anticipation, Shaun scurried on first, spinning dials and hitting gigantic Wonka-esque colorful buttons while checking his watch and pulling on his hat, an action exclusively

reserved for theatrically implying stress. Rarely do you see someone waiting for a slow bus pull down on a top hat.

Shaun played it like a pantomime. He slapped both hands on
his cheeks, turned to the crowd and said in an urgent whisper,
"He's coming!"

Drums rolled on the soundtrack, and jets of rock-star flame
welcomed Rylan's entrance. It was real flame: the heat flushed
my cheeks and I could smell what I thought was gunpowder. Onstage, Rylan bowed, lifted his own top hat, shook it, and transformed it into a Santa hat, which he tucked smugly onto his head.

I returned to my phone. Juliette had sent another text. It was,
of all things, a laughing face emoji. I sent her a question mark.

> Juliette: Of course you should have gone, you idiot.

> Me: You're not mad?

> Juliette: Please stop reducing me to a cliché. First of
> all, I trust you. Second, Erin is family. Of course we
> should help her.

> Me: So you're not mad?

> Juliette: I'm seething, Ern.

Onstage, Rylan had entered a box, which Shaun was systemati-
cally piercing with swords. I could relate.

> Juliette: What makes you think it's okay not to tell
> me something like this? A murder? You could be
> putting yourself in danger. And on Christmas!

Me: You just said I should help Erin.

Juliette: I said WE should help Erin.

Rylan was now producing and disappearing doves at whim. I imagined Juliette's phone screen cracking under the force of her tapping fingers.

Juliette: Remind me how you've solved so many murders with this level of perception?

Me: I'm better at death than life, I guess.

There was a hiss to my right, at the end of the aisle. I turned to see Sam beckoning me. The man beside me cleared his throat unsubtly as I squeezed out of the row and followed Sam up the aisle. It seemed Josh had finagled himself a ticket after all; he sat in the back row, his camera propped on his shoulder. He kept one hand over it, but the glow of the little red light between his fingers betrayed his illegal filming to me, if not the ushers.

The theater had double doors—like a spacecraft air lock—to dull noise bleed, and Sam waited for me between them. I kept the interior door open with my foot to keep an eye on the show. Onstage, Rylan was sawing Theresa in half.

"Something's going on," she whispered urgently. "You're a detective, right?"

"Sort of."

"Well, have you figured it out yet?" She bounced on her toes, more nervous than a bloke with a toupee on a skydive. "The murder?"

I couldn't tell if she was more worried about telling me something or being seen doing so. I understood, of course. People burning to tell secrets in mysteries tend to have an expiry date.

I mentally ran through everything I'd found so far. From Erin's insistence on her terrible alibi, the conundrum of how someone covered her hands in blood without her knowledge, to Lyle calling in his own murder a day early, to his apparent twilight visit to the theater before he died, to the various players at the theater, to the fact that Rylan and his management wanted to buy out the foundation, and finally, to Lyle's body, the bloodied word on the kitchen tiles and the needle mark on his arm.

Onstage, Rylan held up a bullet. "This is a real bullet." He bent into the front row. "May I give it to you, sir, to examine? You ever fired a gun before? You're not a cop, are you? Good. Have you seen a real bullet before? You're a farmer? So you've got guns? Pig shooting? Okay, okay, I've seen *Wolf Creek*—" *Pause for laughs*. "Can you confirm it's a real bullet? As far as you know? That's good enough for me. Thank you, perfect, if I could have that back. Ladies and gentlemen, we have confirmed this is a real, and therefore lethal, bullet."

Shaun handed him a long-barreled revolver, the six-shooter type best suited to a cowboy. I watched for their hands to cross over: wanting to see the palming off of the real bullet for the wax one. Even though I knew what the trick was, it still looked like Rylan held the same bullet.

Rylan clicked the bullet into the chamber of the gun. He held it up for the crowd to see as the ammunition slid in. Shaun wheeled over a table fitted with a clockwork series of cogs, and Rylan placed the gun in the contraption. On the other side of the stage, Theresa wheeled out the device I'd seen on the green room television: a wooden guillotine, a gleaming silver blade hanging from the top.

Rylan walked over to the guillotine, ran his middle finger along the edge of the blade. He theatrically winced at the sharpness and sucked his finger, which got a little nervous chuckle from the crowd. There's something about the darkness of a theater that makes one almost believe anything: that we're in 1776, or the Jellicle Ball, or that a magician is about to put his life at risk.

Rylan got on his knees and let Theresa secure the stocks around his neck with two old-fashioned maritime padlocks, then handcuff his hands behind his back. "I have two minutes to escape these stocks before that blade drops," he announced. An LCD screen lit up in the center of the stage, with a bright red timer reading 2:00. "I can pick the handcuffs, and these two locks either side of my neck, but here's the problem: if I raise the stock, the gun will fire." Shaun cranked a handle, and the revolver pointed down to Rylan. "So my choice is simple: risk my neck with the guillotine or"—he paused dramatically—"catch a bullet in my teeth."

"Well?" Sam in my ear brought me back. The countdown onstage started. 2:00. 1:59.

"I'm sorry." I shook my head. "I have no idea who killed Lyle Pearse."

"Not *Pearse*."

Her eyes bulged, in implication and frustration, then she huffed and dashed out to the foyer. I lingered, one foot toward chasing after her, one eye back on the stage.

Not Pearse.

I chose. I ran back into the theater, to the nearest usher. "You need to stop the show."

"Now?" The usher snorted. "It's the big finale."

1:45. 1:44.

"Immediately."

"Why?"

"Someone's trying to kill Rylan Blaze."

1:39. 1:38.

"That's not funny, sir."

"Trust me. Someone's switched the bloody bullets."

CHAPTER 12

1:30. 1:29.

I ran down the aisle, shouting for the show to halt, waving my arms in the air. On a scale between "kicking up a fuss" and "causing a ruckus," I was well past ruckus. At first, I was met with a tsunami of shh-ing, but as my hollering made it to the stage, Shaun and Theresa turned to peer into the darkness of the audience, trying to find the source of the commotion. Rylan shook his head in annoyance and kept fiddling with his cuffs.

1:25. 1:24.

My logic hinged on the motive for Lyle's murder, which I currently didn't have. You may be snorting, reader, at the predictability of it all. *The bullets*, I suspect you'll smugly say to your partner, clicking off the bedside light, remembering that my view of the prop table had been obstructed and when my sightline cleared, one of the bullets had been knocked over, *of course it's the bullets*. That is, of course, the only element of Rylan's show that he's described as dangerous, and you've seen him confuse a wax bullet and a fatal one already. You've been waiting for this moment.

I climbed up onto the stage, having to wriggle on my belly.

"Get off my stage!" Rylan yelled.

Shaun rushed over to me, confusion in his eyes.

"Someone's switched the bullets," I said, pointing to the device in which the revolver was secured, aimed squarely at Rylan's immobilized head.

1:05. 1:04.

"That's not funny," Shaun said darkly.

"I'm not joking." I lowered my voice so the auditorium couldn't hear. "Stop the show right now. Someone's put a real bullet in the gun."

There was a murmur through the crowd. Rylan, who'd overheard, started swearing, bucking against his restraints.

0:54. 0:53.

"Get me out of this blasted thing," Rylan spat. He was wriggling around, hadn't yet got out of the handcuffs behind his back. He tilted his head up to Shaun. "And take the bullet out of the bloody gun, just to be sure."

"It's mechanical, the gun is locked in place. It has to run the sequence."

"Who designed this shit?"

Shaun turned to me. "It sounds backwards but it's a safety feature. The"—he mouthed the next word in case the audience heard it—"*wax* is only safe after a certain distance. Close up it may as well be a bullet. So the gun locks in. Can't move it, can't access the ammo chamber."

Just as he said this, Rylan seemed to grow a new pair of arms. His hands remained cuffed behind his back, but two additional arms emerged from his torso and started fiddling with the stocks. I realized Rylan's entire back was a shell, like a cicada. He was hiding underneath his own fake body.

0:40. 0:39.

People laughed nervously, still trying to figure out if this was real, or if I was an audience plant and the panic was all part of the act. The spotlights heated the back of my neck and I'd started to sweat. Assumedly, panic *was* part of the planned trick. Rylan would run out of time and the guillotine *would* indeed drop.

That's why he had a fake head. I didn't know at which point the gun was supposed to fire or the blade to drop, but my assumption was everything would happen together when the timer hit zero.

Rylan had unfastened the two padlocks holding his head in place. His octopus-looking self made to lift the stocks.

"Wait!" Shaun yelled. "It's still pointed at you. If you raise the stocks, it'll fire. They're linked."

"Well then move the damn table!" Rylan yelled back.

I didn't need to look at the crowd to know they'd turned from intrigued to concerned: the hiss of whispering filled the room. I ran over to Theresa. "Put something in front of him," I said, "in case it does go off." She stared blankly back at me. "Something heavy that can stop a bullet. Does any part of the set move? Any doors or panels?" This twigged something in her; she appeared to wake up, and she hurried into the wings.

Rylan was peppering the theater with expletives, commands and begging, his voice growing more and more desperate.

Theresa wheeled the box in which she had been sawed in half between Rylan and the gun barrel. It was an optimistic blockade, since it seemed to be made of plywood, but at least it was something.

Sam, watching from the wings, must have thought the same thing. She ran out onstage and stood in front of the gun herself.

0:21. 0:20.

"No!" Theresa grabbed at her sister, but Sam swatted her off. They grappled. Twisting around, one in front of the gun, then the other.

Suddenly, Christopher ran down the aisle and hauled himself up on the stage. "Shaun!" he shouted. "Let's move the table. Just point it away from him, even a few inches."

"It's locked into the stage tracks," Shaun despaired.

"Put your back into it, then." Christopher braced himself in place beside the device and heaved against it with his shoulder. There was a creak of wood, but nothing budged. Shaun added his weight to the second push. This time there was a louder groan, from both men and plywood, but still no movement. And then my easily distracted seat neighbor clambered up onstage. Others followed in a rush. On the next heave there was a splintering sound and, finally, the table moved an inch. The crowd roared its approval. I dared a glance out at the theater: half of the audience were standing, half were covering their faces. Flick was on the phone.

0:15. 0.14.

Sam won the tussle with Theresa, knocking her older sister to the floor.

"Let me do this," Sam said firmly. Theresa stopped scrambling to get up off the floor. She shook her head, eyes red.

The scrum gave another heave, and with the loudest screech so far the table moved again, at least a foot this time. It looked like enough of an angle away from Rylan's head. The audience erupted in applause. Rylan was crying in relief. He went to move the stocks, but Christopher yelled, "Wait! We don't know exactly where the gun's pointed. We have to make sure everyone else is clear."

0:10. 0.09.

"Are you serious?" Rylan gripped the stocks. "I'm about to get my head blown off."

"The gun's not pointed at you anymore, we moved it," Shaun said. He squinted in the direction of the gun, then beckoned Sam and Theresa downstage, out of the line of fire. Sam collapsed into her sister's arms.

"I'm still in a fucking guillotine!" Rylan yelled.

Shaun shouted across the stage, "Relax. I built the thing. It's made of paper, remember. It's not going to do any damage. But as soon as we move the latches, a *real* gun will fire. And that could ricochet, or any number of things. You're safer there until we figure this out."

"Tell that to my finger," Rylan said, flipping him the bird.

0:05. 0:04.

I realize I haven't explained the deductions in full yet, so let me return to the key: motive. Lyle called in a murder that hadn't happened the day before his own. I thought it was odd that he was prophesizing his own death. But he must have stumbled upon a *different* murder plot. Someone in this theater was planning to kill Rylan Blaze by switching the bullets and making it look like an accident. Lyle Pearse found out about the plot and was killed before he could reveal it. Was this why he'd possibly gone to the theater in the early hours of December 21? Was this what Sam had also found out, and tried to tell me?

As per the rules of mysteries, the deductions, logic and conclusions were all sound. Which is all to say that I still can't really blame myself for being wrong.

0:01. 0:00.

The paper guillotine dropped.

THUNK.

For the second time that day, Rylan Blaze's head rolled toward my feet.

To:
DINESH ROY

From:
SHHHHH

CHAPTER 13

Rylan's real head looked just as surprised as his fake one to be separated from his shoulders.

The sound of glass breaking echoed as people dropped their champagne glasses and the auditorium erupted first into screams, and then to a thunder of footsteps as the audience stampeded to the doors. I glanced out into the melee. Flick was helping guide people to the exits, trying to prevent a crush. Christopher was going around checking on everyone onstage. Shaun stumbled over and vomited into the sawn-in-half box. Sam had her head in her hands, while Theresa stood frozen in shock, save for her shaking antlers. Rylan's Santa hat had been knocked off in the chop and lay, limp, at the base of the guillotine. I'd seen dead bodies before, hell, I'd seen real-life murders. But never something of this sudden violence.

No one spoke until the theater was empty of audience. Aside from, I couldn't help but notice, a shadow in the back of the stalls accompanied by a little red light. The stage lights were brutally hot, and the heat shining onto the blood filled the air with an iron tang, which crept into my nostrils and clung to the top of my throat. As if reading my mind, the spotlight lowered, sliding down the stage and over the backs of the seats. That meant Dinesh had left the lighting booth, dropping the spotlight on his way out.

"No one touch anything," I said, because it seemed like the right thing to say, not because people were actually reaching for corpses or heads. I pulled one of the drapes off the set and laid it over Rylan's head. Thankfully, the fake body-shell and cloak had collapsed over Rylan's real one. There was a surprisingly small puddle of blood. This is a Christmas story, after all.

The guillotine's blade was currently buried in the stocks, a strip of gleaming silver at the top, a similar blood-spattered inch of silver out the bottom. I could tell there was a slot all the way through the stocks; if the blade hadn't been attached to a rope it could have gone right through and hit the floor. The guillotine frame itself, under the oak-styled paint job, was cheap balsa wood. A little handle on the side winched the blade back up to the top by a pulley system. I wrapped my hand in my shirt and turned it. The bloodied silver sheet emerged.

"Paper?" I said, turning to Shaun, who was wiping his mouth with the back of his hand. "Seriously?"

Shaun was so pale it seemed he'd lost the second highest amount of blood onstage. I reminded myself not everyone had seen as many dead bodies as I had, and waited for him to compose himself and walk over. When he did, he reached out and grabbed the blade by the sides, taking care to touch a non-blood-spattered section. He must have registered my surprise, because he turned to me and said, "My fingerprints are on it anyway, I built the damn thing. Besides, it's not the murder weapon. Metallic paint and the lighting make it look real but this thing wouldn't give you a paper-cut." He tore the blade a couple of inches, easily. "See?"

"It did give him a paper-cut, actually," I said absentmindedly, looking over Rylan's body. *Tell that to my finger*, Rylan had shouted in those final seconds. I'd thought it was merely anger, but he'd been complaining that the blade was sharp.

"This isn't a nick to the finger. It just cut his freaking *head off*," Theresa screamed.

Shaun put his hands in the air. "I don't know what to tell you!

You saw what I saw. So it gave him a paper-cut. It's still only *paper*. Rylan knew that: he still got in the trick."

"You worked on the device before the show," I said to Theresa. "I saw it on the green room television screen."

Sam's eyes went wide with fear for her sister. Theresa folded her arms indignantly. "What are you accusing me of?"

"Nothing," I said magnanimously. "I'm asking if you thought anything was wrong when you checked it before the show."

"It's not my job to check it." Theresa jabbed a finger at Shaun. "That's his job. I just dust it. I didn't tamper with it."

"And you're saying *I* did?" Shaun took a step toward Theresa.

I jumped between them to intervene just as the doors to the theater clattered open and two police officers entered, accompanied by a wave of baking heat. The lead officer wore plain clothes and, judging by his rosy-red cheeks, had been summoned from a bar, likely already off for his holiday. The officer following was female, and the fact she was wearing a uniform at all, and hence working so close to Christmas, indicated her junior position.

As if they were part of the show, the lead officer came to a stop directly in the downward-pointing spotlight. He clicked his fingers and the junior officer scurried over to Josh Felman. I couldn't hear what she was saying, but she was pointing at his GoPro, and I could surmise that she was asking for the footage.

The lead bloke put his hands on his hips and took a deep breath through his nose. He had a pockmarked face that looked like several people had put their cigarettes out on it. "Senior Sergeant Sullivan," he said. "I'd say pleasure to meet you all but two murders in one day is too many in my town." I struggled not to roll my eyes: a *my town* kind of cop. "Now, it's four days from Christmas and this much carnage is bound to give our holding cells a workout. Luckily, our killer has some respect for the police force's carbon footprint, as our forensics crew from Sydney are still up here from this morning's murder. They're on the way over here as we speak. So for now, everyone clear off the stage. None of you can leave until I get statements, fingerprints and whatever else you want to cough up. And I'll need a ticketing report to track down the audience that was here. Capiche?" He pronounced it wrong, more like *ceviche*. "Except for you, Cunningham. Oh, don't act surprised, I know who you are. And that journo." He thumbed to the back of the room, at Josh. "Out."

I opened my mouth to protest, but he folded his arms. I could tell the next discussion would be about interfering with a crime scene—*his* crime scene. I chose not to pursue it and hopped off the stage.

"I saw as much as anyone here," I said. "I even tried to stop it."

"My apologies," Sullivan sniffed. "I didn't realize he'd been shot in the head like you thought. I assumed he'd been decapitated." His gaze wavered theatrically to the two draped lumps on the stage. "Oh! Well, what do you know."

"I can help," I said, petulant. "Rylan's company was offering on the business side of the foundation—the real estate, these theaters—that's a whopper of a deal. That possibly ties both murders together."

"It might. Luckily, we've already got a killer in our cells. I believe you know her pretty well."

"Why on earth would Erin want to stop a real-estate deal?"

"That is *my* job to find out. Not yours."

I thought about my options and chose the path of least resistance. "Your town, your suspects," I acquiesced. I was tempted to throw in an artificial bow, but thought it was overkill.

As I passed him, Josh was bickering about handing over his recordings, so I was first outside. The night was searing, without a lick of breeze for relief. Heat from the sun is one thing, but a still night is like a blanket pressed over you. I felt vacuum-packed into my own skin. The summer cicadas chirped with their papery rattle in the treetops, and filled the air with static. The stars were gems in the navy sky.

The parking lot was dotted with the remaining seven civilian cars and a police cruiser. This fit my number of suspects currently inside the theater. Factor in a victim, however, and the number of vehicles in the lot appeared to be one short.

Someone had left.

I realized that, after I'd seen the spotlight droop, Dinesh hadn't come into the auditorium. I didn't want to jump to conclusions, but the fact he was so quick to leave was ominous. I planned to ask him just that. The problem was, I had no idea where Dinesh lived, and while I've solved a few murders these last few years, I've never had to really gumshoe a missing person. It wasn't in my skill set.

Then I saw a bicycle tied to a tree. Which meant that we *did* have the correct number of vehicles for people. Dinesh was still here. Just not inside the theater.

While the stillness of the night was torture for the temperature, it also meant that sound carried far.

That's why it was so clear when, deep in the bush, I heard a scream.

PUDDLE

CHAPTER 14

I crashed into the bush at a sprint. Clawed fingertips of branches reached for my arms, and the uneven, rocky ground treated my ankles like a tetherball game, slapping them back and forth.

It's well known that you shouldn't walk into the bush without a plan. It only takes a few steps for the arching branches to close off the sky above, and the thickness of trees to seem like they pull up roots and shuffle in, making a labyrinth that rotates the walls every time you turn around. Direction has its suitcases packed by the door, Hope has the engine on in the car outside. Search parties have found bodies, dead from dehydration, meters from highways. Imagine dying, thinking no one will ever find you, when you're a thicket of branches away from a McDonald's parking lot and a cheeseburger.

All this to say that if getting lost in the day is terrifying, it is doubly so at night.

My phone flashlight bounced off the gum trees as I moved in what I hoped was the direction of the scream. Not only is physical direction compromised in the bush, but sound plays tricks on your ears too. The lookout is called Echo Point for a reason. Noise bounces off the rocks and gullies. Someone can say something to your face and you'd think they were behind you.

I moved as fast as I trusted myself to. My light would occasionally flick over something animal that would shoot away into the scrub with a rustle of leaves. Dozens of glinting bright spots—marsupial eyes—shone from above. The whole place was alive.

A gleam in my torchlight caught my eye. Something metal, man-made.

"Dinesh?" I called, edging forward. I had to be careful; I could break a leg or split my head open if I took a spill. Worse still, I could saunter straight off a cliff. The drops off the Katoomba plateau were up to three hundred meters. You'd never even know you were dead until the wind whistled past your ears.

The ground transformed from dirt to rock, and I moved more slowly, thinking I was nearing an edge. Nature and night might hide clifftops and snakes, but it could also hide men. Dinesh could have left something on a precipice and be waiting for me to bend to pick it up. Two hands in the back was all it would take. Depending on the cliff, it could be years until my body was found.

A flutter in the trees behind, leaves and nuts falling, defibrillated me. I spun. My torch showed nothing but trees and eyes.

I turned back and inched closer. The glinting object was a pair of glasses. They were propped up on a pair of neatly laced shoes. This bizarre assembly was perched on the rock, just before the ground fell away into an abyss so deep my flashlight dissolved into blackness.

I pulled back from the ledge, legs jellied from the height, but no longer scared of being rushed from the bushes. The neatly placed shoes, the glasses, angled up to reflect the light. It was obvious. That was the whole point. I pictured Dinesh, snot-blotched face, calmly tying his shoes, placing his glasses gently down, standing tall and leaning forward to give himself to the crater below.

But detective and mystery reader alike must always remember something: no body, no death. If you don't see a corpse, you can bet your bottom dollar that person's coming back. It's happened to me twice now in my previous cases, and I sure wasn't falling for it again.

"Dinesh." I turned to face the quiet bushel of tree trunks. "Guilty men jump. Scared men hide." There was no response from the thicket. I doubled down. The storytelling was too obvious. In 1957, a man named Vere Gordon Childe left his hat, compass, pipe and glasses on a clifftop in the Blue Mountains and fell to his death. Dinesh was aping this story. Who would stage such an audacious and public murder, and then crumble and throw themselves to their end? The reason I knew he was scared was the other side of the coin: Who would fake a suicide just to avoid a couple of questions from not-even-a-real-detective? "You're not running from me though, are you? Who are you afraid of?"

A voice came from the dark. I couldn't tell if it was left, right or in front of me.

"I don't know. But that's the whole point."

FLEE

CHAPTER 15

Dinesh's face, ragged with anguish, emerged from the bushes to my left. He blinked incessantly without his glasses. He was barefoot, leaves and mud caked to his toes.

"Just leave me out of it." He sniffed. "I didn't kill anyone."

"I don't think you did," I said. "But you're worried about being next on someone's list. I think Lyle was killed because he knew something about today. And I think you're worried that you might be another loose end. That's why you screamed, made it look like you jumped."

In my experience, people confronted with a lie are overwhelmingly belligerent. But there is always a glimmer of relief that they no longer have to keep up the charade. Dinesh, however, was only showing the latter. He softened. "Look, I don't know what happened to Lyle. And I don't know what the hell happened with the guillotine. Isn't it supposed to be made of paper? I don't know anything."

"And yet you ran?"

"Someone's killing people who they think know *something*."

"What do they think you know?"

"Not as much as I thought. I don't know who killed Rylan, if that's your next question."

"You were running from someone, and you didn't know who it was?"

"I was unlocking my bike when I heard someone come out of the theater. I figured, whoever it was, it was best if I bought myself some time. If it was the killer, there's no point chasing after a dead man. I didn't know it was you until you stepped into the moonlight by the edge. You're the fella that stopped the show. Who are you?"

"I'm a—" I hesitated. What was I, exactly? I'm hardly a private eye. "A very *public* detective."

"How'd you know about the bullets?"

"I didn't," I said honestly. Though Sam had pointed me in the right direction. She'd been anxious, I remembered. But was it more than that? Fear? Was she trying to help me catch a killer for the same reason Dinesh wanted to run away? "I was right about the murder but wrong about the method."

Dinesh ground his jaw. He wasn't the type of suspect to monologue, so I decided to do it for him.

"I think this has something to do with the twelfth of December. You were pulled off the tour. Sam told me she chartered a jet to get Rylan here and still make the show that night in Toowoomba. You, Rylan and Lyle had a meeting that day. And now two out of three people in that meeting are dead."

Dinesh looked at the ground.

"Senior Sergeant Sullivan showed up just now and you ran. Let me see if I've got this right. One, Lyle's heavy pyramid trophy is misaligned with the rest of the display and there's a hole in his office drywall. Two, Rylan Blaze told me the staff here were *thieving bastards*. Three, you've had a run in with the police before."

I tossed Dinesh his glasses, and he slid them on. He looked exhausted, which, in detective terms, means ready to talk. I decided to ask him straight:

"Lyle Pearse fired you on December twelfth, didn't he?"

15

FIRED

To:

SHAUN MARTIN

From:

SANTA

CHAPTER 16

You could have replaced all the flashing baubles on any Christmas tree with the way the twenty-four-hour motel attendant's eyes lit up when I told him I needed a last-minute booking and was paying cash. He pretended to squeeze me in, dragging his pencil down an empty booking sheet and tutting, and I played along with the charade, paying the inflated rate with equally fake gratitude.

If the clerk had paid *me,* I would have overpaid for the room, I thought, as I lay on top of the itchy, pilled blanket that was so thin it seemed it was missing its true calling as a bridal veil. Not that it mattered in the heat. An air conditioner had coughed so much black dust into the room I'd had to turn it off. I had a water-soaked tea towel across my brow instead. Christmas Day was forecast to be a scorcher, and the mercury was starting the climb. I hoped I'd be back home by then. White Christmases can go jump, in my opinion. Give me a backyard pool and a recycling bin with spray-painted cricket stumps on it any day.

The truth was, I was fantasizing about a normal Christmas because my brain was overstimulated from everything that had happened. I'd only been in town for six hours, and I'd already seen two dead bodies (granted, one was photographed). This was, even for me, an efficient amount of carnage.

But this was the third case I've investigated, and lying on the bed, still pondering the meaning of everything I'd seen, I was humbled by one inescapable fact: every time I try to solve a murder, someone else dies along the way. Of course, this is a murder mystery staple: the midpoint murder (or the "second ad-break murder" if you want to think about television) both props up the reader's interest and moves the plot along. But in real life it doesn't seem fair. I couldn't shake the feeling that, as much as I solved these cases, people were dying because I wasn't solving them fast enough.

Images stayed on the backs of my eyelids: a big blue unopened Secret Santa present for Rylan Blaze; four unopened doors for Lyle Pearse. Half-finished projects from half-finished lives.

I couldn't sleep. I tried to turn over what Dinesh had told me, much of which I'd already surmised and he'd simply confirmed. He'd nodded slowly on my question of his firing. Apparently Rylan Blaze had reported to Pearse that Dinesh had stolen something, and a peridot-jeweled ring was swiftly found teleported, if Dinesh was to be believed, from Rylan's dressing room to Dinesh's bag. Pearse had promptly fired Dinesh, despite his protestations of innocence.

"I didn't even know what I was accused of stealing. I didn't know Rylan's ring had been found in my stuff until Flick told me later that was the reason. Cokehead probably lost it, if you ask me. Which no one did, by the way. No such thing as a fair hearing to an ex-junkie. Time for me to *explore other opportunities*, they said. I overreacted, throwing that damn trophy, and I was marched out by security." He'd kicked a rock, and I'd heard it clatter off the cliff-face and crash into the treetops below a full seven seconds later. My stomach levitated as I pictured the height. "So much for second chances."

"Why were you on tonight?" I'd asked.

"New guy was sick. I'm the only one who knows the cues. And I can see what you're thinking. I would have loved to stick it to them. But I got no severance. I charged Flick triple for the night; she said yes. I didn't steal squat, but I am taking their money."

Dinesh did, indeed, have motives for both murders: the man who fired him, and the man whose fault it was. Even so, I believed him. I didn't think his fear, when I'd chased him through the bush, was possible to manufacture.

I put Dinesh's firing and trophy-throwing in the too-hard basket and begrudgingly emailed Josh. I wanted to know more about Lyle's needle mark and was hoping he had a police contact bribable enough to send through any blood-testing reports on Lyle and Erin. After the email had swooshed away, I watched YouTube clips of Lyle accepting awards and presenting university graduation speeches. He talked about his brother's death, how he wanted to help people surpass society's expectations of them, and closed every speech with the phrase: *Passion creates change.* I tried to reconcile this man with the needle mark in his arm.

An email from Josh landed. *Will try and get those reports. Check it out though.* I clicked on the link he'd included. The auditorium filled my screen. Josh had managed to upload his footage to a private server before the police had confiscated it.

Onstage was absolute chaos. Shaun and I arguing, Rylan yelling from the stocks. Sam placing herself in front of the gun barrel, Theresa pulling her away. Then members of the audience, alongside Shaun and Christopher, straining against the set. I replayed the blade falling in slow motion twice and then paused the video, somewhat squeamishly, at the moment when Rylan's head, to put it nicely, *explored other opportunities* from his body. There was the paper blade, buried in the stocks, which I'd removed and Shaun had torn later. Beneath the stocks was a gap of clear air, through which I could see the rest of Rylan's body, before the stage floor. I'd wondered if there could be a second, hidden, blade. But where did it go? I couldn't see anything at all in the frames, rolling the video back and forth. Let alone something that could have scythed through Rylan's neck.

Writing this all out on Christmas Day, I have the strange perspective of feeling like I am looking down on myself, sweating a patch on that prison bunk of a motel bed, perplexed, anguished and a little bit lonely. I watch myself send a text message to Juliette. I watch myself finally dip into sleep, only to be woken by the imagined THUNK of a falling guillotine. I wish I could lean into my own narrative here and tell myself that I do indeed solve the crime, a feat that will be accompanied by both being shot in the chest and witnessing another death. I'd tell myself that I will, eventually, be writing it all out with shortbread in one hand and a pen in the other.

But motel-me, dawn-hours-of-December-22-me, doesn't yet know the solution to two impossible murders. A woman covered in blood who doesn't remember how it got on her. And a man decapitated . . . by a piece of paper.

While the first was puzzling, the second was downright fantastical. There was no denying what everyone in the theater had seen: The blade had come down, and Rylan's head had come off. Then I'd personally raised the very same blade, to find it nothing but flimsy paper, easily torn in Shaun's hand. I'd seen it with my own eyes.

Then again, that was the whole point of a magic trick, wasn't it?

The clattering of my phone woke me. I swiped it without looking and was surprised to hear Erin on the other end. The line was crackling, reception tarnished by the bowels of steel and concrete from which the call was made.

"I heard about Rylan Blaze," she said.

"You're allowed a call this early?"

"Officer let me borrow their phone for an emergency. Besides, it's Christmas." She sounded upbeat. A whole different person from the ragged, bloody woman who'd sat across from me the day before. "Another murder, which I clearly couldn't have committed. This clears me, right?"

I hesitated. I could almost hear her deflate.

"Right?" she asked again.

"Sorry, Erin." I rubbed sleep from my eyes. "I wish it did. But it only clears you if we can confirm that Lyle and Rylan both have the same killer." I heard a thud on the phone, and pictured Erin slapping the device against her forehead. "It looks like Rylan's death was orchestrated in advance. The guillotine could have been tampered with anytime yesterday. Before that, even. I wish I could lie to you that it was good news. I'm sorry. Reliable narrator here." I squeezed my eyes tightly shut. Erin's and my marriage had been a disaster. The problems hadn't started with my first dead body, covered in spiderwebs, all those years ago, but that was part of it. And then the murders that followed, that Cunningham name strapped to her like an anchor. Lyle had helped her leave it behind. Now he was gone and here I was, dragging her back, bodies piling up, like none of it had ever changed. "Maybe I'm not right for this," I said eventually. "I'm not a professional. I could wind up doing more damage here."

"You know why I called you?" She said it softly. "I'm not going to tell you I couldn't have done it. I didn't do that yesterday, and I'm not now. Because after what happened on the mountain, after the murders. All that death." She made a retching sound. "I scrub my hands raw. I feel like Lady Macbeth, stained."

"Maybe don't reference Lady Macbeth when you're trying to assert your innocence." I tried for levity and missed by an ocean.

"I'm not asserting anything. What if . . . all the things I've seen. What if something snapped? What if I *did* do this? I called you not because I wanted you to prove me innocent." The phone crackled. "I hope you do. Every fiber in me *hopes* you do. But I woke up covered in blood, Ernest. And I . . . I don't know if I killed him or not. That's what I want you to find out. Am I a killer? Am I capable of this?"

"You aren't," I said softly. "I know you."

"That's the problem." She was fighting back tears. "How can you? I don't even know myself."

CHAPTER 17

Katoomba is so high it sits above the morning clouds. This early, just before seven, wisps of mist and dew hung in the air. Floating asteroids of rock emerged from the fluffy meringue. The sun had begun its quest to burn the clouds to vapor, but hadn't quite won, so the morning was steamy.

Lyle and Erin's home was nearer to town than the theater, out by an old sanatorium-turned-hotel named the Hydro Majestic. It's funny how the most prized modern real estate is situated on the bones of trauma. We used to send the insane to the mountains while we stayed in the cities. Now the cities drive us insane and we try to escape to the mountains.

Josh Felman was efficient, I have to admit. As I was walking up the drive my phone buzzed with an email from him, a few documents attached: toxicology reports on Erin and Lyle, and a list of items the police had taken from the house as evidence. The body of the email was a short message: *Both clean. Shame. Would have been a story.*

That was one theory squashed. But I now had a different question: If Pearse was clean, why did he have a needle mark in his arm?

I was also annoyed, unfairly, by just how damn helpful Josh Felman was being. So much for a nemesis.

Erin and Lyle's home was a cubic mansion, which looked to be assembled of slate-gray rectangular prisms balanced (I would suggest precariously) on top of one another. Like an actor that's overdone it on the plastic surgery, it looked enormously expensive and was astoundingly ugly. The blue and white police tape across the door at least gave the place some personality.

I stepped onto the front porch, glanced at the lantern affixed nearby at head height, and patted around the top of it until I found a grimy key, exactly where Erin and I used to hide our own. The door showed no sign of forced entry. No windows were broken along the front of the house. The key's filth meant it hadn't been used, either with or without permission. That meant the killer had been let into the house. Or lived there. I unlocked the door.

Heat is not kind to blood or nostrils. The stench hit me as soon as I opened the door, rotten and fleshy, like coming home from holiday to discover the fridge is out. In front of me, down the hall, I recognized the staircase from the forensic photos, splotched with stains leading up (or down), just as Erin had described. The only difference was the blood was older, the bright red of its oxygen expunged, and now a treacle-brown.

I could tell by the smell that the kitchen was on the right, so I hooked to the left, through a dining room and into a living room, where a leafless Christmas tree stood sentry, spray-painted gold and without a lick of green or ornament: the type of minimalistic style to which the rich are accustomed. Four small presents sat under the tree, delicately wrapped, none bigger than my fist. The ground floor also had a wine cellar, a cheese room (which smelled worse than the blood, to be honest), a guest bedroom and an elevator. Erin had definitely upgraded.

I made my way into the kitchen and was immediately surprised by how preserved the crime scene was. Erin had been right: forensics clear a crime scene and then just hand it back to the owner to scrub up themselves. The rest of the murders I've been involved with have been, to put it simply, on the go. Takeaway. So I was both surprised and relieved to see that everything was as in the pictures, sans Lyle's body.

I stepped carefully around the pool of blood—larger than Rylan's, but Lyle was a bigger guy, does that make you bleed more? I had no idea—and his scrawled, blood-written final message: *Christmas*. Those familiar, randomly sized letters—the giant *h*, the stumpy *t*—like a child's school poster project where they've started the font size too energetically and run out of room. It still meant nothing to me. Why waste your last moment writing the holiday? Why not write something useful? Like: *Erin is innocent*. Or, as I know some of you are probably thinking but it hasn't occurred to me yet, your computer password.

The knife block was missing. I checked my email: it was on Felman's list of evidence items the police had taken. The murder weapon was indeed Erin's knife. I scanned the benches, the sink, the garbage (empty, also taken by forensics), and the fridge, on which was stuck a Post-it note (*Bread + Milk*) in Lyle's handwriting, which I knew purely because I didn't recognize it as Erin's. Trying to decide if the Post-it note was a clue (it is), I checked inside the fridge: indeed, they had no milk. A near-finished loaf of bread lay by the toaster. So it's a clue, but not, like, a secret code or anything. Bread means bread and milk means milk.

I turned back into the hall and sidestepped up the stairs so as not to tread on the blood. There was a larger stain on the landing where the knife had lain. It definitely appeared, from the drips, that the knife had been carried upstairs after the murder, rather than Lyle's being stabbed upstairs and stumbling down into the kitchen. Which did no favor to debunking the theory that Erin had murdered her partner in the kitchen and then simply went back to bed, dropping the knife along the way.

I didn't think Erin was lying about her lack of recollection. I found myself wondering if anyone could be capable of committing such a crime and yet have no memory of it. Josh's email said her blood was clean as well as Lyle's, and the toxicology report backed that up: there was a carnival of the word *undetected* on both forms, and the final page included the phrase *No sedatives*. How else can you erase someone's memories?

Josh had told me Erin had been struggling with nightmares and sleepwalking as a symptom of her PTSD. She'd told me herself that our experience in the snow had scarred her. *I can barely eat without thinking about the corpses, the stench, their faces.* I wondered if such a thing as traumatic amnesia existed. Could she have seen, or done, something so horrible that she'd deliberately blocked it from her memory?

The top-floor bedroom had been stripped of bedding, which I knew was blood-stained with Erin's handprints. The empty mattress's only sign of the mess was a few tiny brown dots. An unfinished mug, Erin's hot chocolate, sat on the bedside table. The remnants had turned chalky white and were a day away from mold. I picked up the mug, figuring Erin shouldn't have to clean up blood and mold in the same day once I got her out. *If I got her out*, I thought darkly. I shook it away.

I rinsed the mug in the bathroom. There was no soap, so I did my best with water and my fingertips. The bathroom was white tiled, floor to ceiling, and the wall tiles were blemished with tiny freckles of brown, sprayed like the droplets of a sneeze. I flicked the light switch to no avail. Of course, Erin had already told me that: *I did flick the ensuite light but it was busted, didn't come on.* I looked at the ceiling. The light wasn't just busted. It wasn't in the socket at all.

Hang on. What else had Erin said? That she never turned on the bedroom light when she went to the bathroom, so she hadn't known whether Lyle was in bed when she'd got up around one. I thought about that for a second, then examined the light switch. There was no blood on it.

So that meant one thing, which I will tell you as fact, because it is: Erin's hands did not have blood on them when she went to the bathroom.

My mind was still cycling through the possibilities. PTSD. Amnesia. I tried to picture Erin with a knife in her hand and was surprised at how easy it was. I played it in my mind: Erin stabbing Lyle multiple times, and then walking up the stairs in a stupor, the knife slipping from her hands. Lying down, pulling up the bloodied sheets. In one replay she was fast asleep. In the other, her eyes were open. Aware.

It scared me a little. But even picturing her with the knife, my darkest thought was something else: she's a former Cunningham. Everyone in my family has killed someone. If she *had* done this, why hadn't she done a better job of getting away with it?

CHAPTER 18

I'm going to chalk up what happened next as a Christmas miracle. I headed downstairs to place Erin's mug on the kitchen sink. As I stepped into the kitchen the sun was slicing through the windows, making me squint as it glanced off the white marble bench tops. On the floor, past the blood, the ray of light settled in a corner. And there I saw a little twinkle.

It was a blink-and-miss-it clue. I snatched a square of paper towel and coaxed the object out from the corner. It was a small piece of glass, delicate and thin. Too thin to be from a regular water glass, more like an expensive champagne flute or wineglass. Or—I thought about the needle mark in Lyle's arm—a syringe.

I pulled out my phone and checked the inventory from the forensic report. Nowhere on the list of collected evidence was an item made of glass, broken or whole. This shard had been missed by forensics. That made it all the more perplexing. This was a killer who didn't try to cover up the scene. They'd left a body sprawled in the kitchen, a murder weapon on the stairs and blood splattered across both levels of the house. So why in the world had they stopped and cleaned up something like a broken wineglass?

Panel vans get a bad rap, being the vehicle of choice for terrorists and predators, but they really are the vultures of the automobile industry: if you see a flock of them, you know a tragedy lurks nearby. To prove my theory, the theater parking lot was cleared of civilian cars and filled with news vans, as well as a black coroner's one. Of course, a magician cutting off his own head would make national, even international, news. I realized Josh was probably set to make bank selling his secret footage to the highest bidder.

The wisps of cloud had dissipated and it was so bright that I couldn't look at the glinting glass atrium without wincing. A shimmer rose off the black tar of the parking lot. I snuck around the side of the theater, not wanting to have to try to talk my way past the police. The code Sam had given me, 4183, worked on the stage door, and I slipped in, grateful for a blast of air-conditioning down my neck. The second time around, I was better accustomed to the maze of backstage, and headed for upstairs. I could hear voices on the stage, so I walked quickly.

In Lyle's office, I shut the door and lowered the blinds. Everything was the same as I'd left it, which didn't surprise me. Lyle would be low on the suspect list. How could the police suspect a dead man of committing a murder?

Several ideas had coagulated over the last twelve hours: one from watching Lyle's series of speeches and TED Talks last night, and the others while looking at his pool of blood in the kitchen this morning.

I headed to the computer, wiggled the mouse, and was greeted by the familiar log-in screen. Sorry to disappoint those readers expecting me to lean forward and whisper *Christmas* into the microphone. Instead, I got out my phone, loaded up YouTube, and fast-forwarded to the right spot in the video. Then I held up the phone and let Lyle himself say "*Passion creates change.*"

The computer gave a little ribbit of acceptance, and I was in.

And then the door to Lyle's office clicked open, and Christopher Sleet walked in. "What the hell are you doing here?" he said.

CHAPTER 19

I backed away from the computer, focused on Christopher's head tilting out into the corridor as he decided whether or not to call one of the officers downstairs. I wouldn't do Erin much good if I was in a cell next to her. Then Christopher clicked the door shut, flicked the light off and walked over to me.

"Can see the light's on even with the blinds down," he said. "That's how I knew you were in here. Cops are bloody useless, but even they would have figured that one out." He drummed his fingers on the desk next to me. "They've brought us all back in for questioning, but I'm done. How'd you get into the computer?"

His inquisitiveness would usually have twigged my radar, but this was tempered by the fact that, strangely, almost every one of my suspects wanted me close. Flick had invited me in; Felman had given me police files; Sam had tried to warn me about the murder. I'd be a fool to think that, even aside from murder, all these approaches didn't have ulterior motives. Christopher was no different. As the foundation counselor, I figured he probably knew the most about the rest of my suspects, so it was worth indulging him. Plus, he hadn't called the police *or* seemed keen to kill me, two attributes I consider mandatory for conversation.

I turned back to the screen. "Adding computer hacking to my detective repertoire," I said. "We haven't had a chance to talk properly yet. I'm having trouble getting a grasp on who Lyle really was. Behind the foundation stuff. How well did you know him?"

"Very well. He saved—"

"Your life," I finished for him. "Yeah, there's a bit of that going around here."

"That's because it's true. I was one of the Pearse Foundation's first graduates. Lyle and I became good friends. Even outside of the"—he cupped his hands like a beggar—"worship, savior thing. That's why, once I got my degree—which he paid for, by the way—I knew I'd come back and work for him."

"Rarely is such a benevolent man a murder victim," I muttered. Lyle's desktop was methodical and organized, as clean as his actual desk. I opened up his email. Contrary to popular belief, accessing someone's computer doesn't immediately spill all the required information into an investigator's lap. Lyle's email was overwhelmed after just a day in the morgue (I was tempted to put up an out-of-office, but didn't know what to say: *Thank you for your email, apologies but I am currently deceased*).

"What do you mean by that?"

"You're telling me this man had no flaws, no enemies? Dinesh doesn't seem to think he was treated all that fairly."

Christopher faltered. "For the record, I thought that was a bit harsh."

"But you trust Pearse? You believed in him. Or do you just feel obligated because he paid for your degree?"

"Of course I trusted him," Christopher snapped. "And his loyalty was earned. Not bought. I'm here to give people second chances, like Pearse gave me. I want to make a difference."

"Like Pearse used to."

"Used to?"

I spun the monitor around so Christopher could read the email I'd just found.

From: AGarritt@EnigmaEntertainment.com
To: L.Pearse@ThePearseFoundation.org
Date: December 20, 2024, 11:16am
Subject: Final Offer

Rylan told me you're coming around. Good to hear.
17 Million, final offer. All sites, complexes and land. You retain
the name.

As always, reserving rights.

Aidan

And yes, before you complain about the eyesore, I've had to request that this email be reprinted exactly as I saw it. Fair play mystery and all. It tickled me at the time, because Lyle Pearse was certainly the first successful businessman I'd ever seen to use such a goofy font. As it turns out, it's quite important. In keeping with an accidental theme—my first case involved a full stop, my second a comma—this may well be the first mystery ever solved by Comic Sans.

I'd been hoping to trigger a reaction by showing him the email, but Christopher didn't seem bothered. He said, "Good."

"You wouldn't be upset if he sold up?"

"The opposite, actually. I'd be delighted. Read the email again. It's just real estate they're haggling over. Pearse can keep the foundation's name, give a seventeen-million-dollar cash injection into the real work. Price seems fair going the other way, Rylan's team gets state-of-the-art theaters across the country and prime real estate. It sounds like a great idea to me. Flick's the one who's against it."

His answer told me that, while he knew about the possible sale, he hadn't known the details. It loosened me up a little. It's hard to kill over a contract you don't know the contents of. "Now she's in charge, is Flick likely to block the sale?"

Christopher shrugged. "Maybe."

"This sounds like Pearse *had* initially resisted the idea of selling, but something happened that started to change his mind," I offered.

"Seventeen million sounds like a mind-changer to me."

Of course, a number like that is worth killing over, in this or any other mystery, so don't count it out, but that wasn't what I was getting at.

I opened a folder called "Voice Notes." The files were labeled by date and time. I scrolled until I found one labeled *Dec-12–13:48*, and pressed play. I was aware of Christopher at my shoulder, but if, as I suspected, this memo contained details of Dinesh's firing, I figured I might need his opinion.

"*As expected, Dinesh didn't take it well. Flick's advice to rip the bandage off quickly was perceptive, as if I hadn't fired him immediately I don't think I would have got much else out. I didn't even get a chance to lay out the accusation. File incident report with HR, re: violence. Book contractor to patch the hole in the wall. Check severance entitlements with Flick, see if violation of behavioral policy is grounds to void pay-out entitlements.*" A sigh. "*I thought he was one of the good ones. I guess you never know.*"

I looked back up at Christopher. "Flick didn't give me the passcode in front of Sam the other day, and then Pearse fired Dinesh without so much as a fair trial. I didn't spot a lot of foundation kids at the gala, just you and Theresa wheeled out as success stories. None of the current intake were there as guests. Is the foundation really practicing what it preaches?"

Christopher looked like he had a toothache. That Lyle might be losing faith in his own foundation was hard to stomach. "Flick believes that the donors prefer to see what they've helped, not what they're helping, it's true." He hesitated a second. "I disagree, obviously. We use the term *graduate*, but everyone knows you don't just finish up and that's it. Addiction follows you around every damn day. And if the bad stuff stays with you, well, so should the foundation. Everyone needs a second chance. Pearse believed that, I'm sure of it, but he might have felt he needed a hard stance with his buyer on the line. Flick's from a different world. She would have been in Pearse's ear about things like that."

That matched what Flick had told me. Treat a business like a charity and a charity like a business.

If that was the case, why didn't she want to sell? Seventeen million dollars sounded like a good business decision to me.

"Maybe Dinesh stealing Rylan's ring was the final straw for Lyle," I continued. "Someone who'd made their mark, found their *passion*, regressing. Lyle seeing his hard work, the change he believed he was making, undone like that?"

I clicked another voice memo, this one from December 10. Lyle's recorded ghost came back on. *"Just need to get my thoughts in order. This morning, I got a call from Flick. She's found a jeweled ring of Rylan's in Dinesh's bag."* The sound of his fingers drumming on the table. *"I hate that Rylan's right. But . . ."* He swore softly to himself. *"I have to let him go. Sam's organizing travel. I'd rather do it in person."* The recording fizzed; Lyle was too loud, too close to the microphone. *"Meanwhile, Enigma's offer's still on the table. Rylan said it's an opportunity to get out before I get robbed out of house and home. This, of course, after I told him that if I see him with a substance around my graduates again . . ."*

Pearse sounded different here. Brighter, even with the little wavers of uncertainty. The memo he'd made on the twelfth, after Dinesh had thrown one of his trophies through the wall, revealed a much more subdued, disappointed man. I could see why he hadn't been in the mood for chocolate.

I scrolled down the list of voice files. Specifically, I was looking for anything recorded in the dawn hours of the twenty-first, when I suspected Lyle had secretly come into his office. Disappointingly, the last memo was dated the twentieth, in the afternoon. I clicked it.

"*Email to Flick,*" Pearse dictated. He sounded even further from the man in the first recording: unraveled and exhausted. There was a pause, a sniffle of breath: he was close to the mic. "*I'm going to sell. What I've built . . . I know you don't want to, that you still think we're doing good work. But I've seen the rotten core. I know it's hard to hear. We aren't helping anyone, so it's time to help ourselves. You'll get dividends, of course. The offer's very generous as it is, but I think I can tilt it up. Send.*" There was a muffled sound as Pearse moved about. Then he spoke again, this time farther from the microphone. "*Hello? Is this a person or a robot? Can whoever gets this call me back immediately?*" I realized he was talking on the phone and must not have realized the memo was still recording. "*I'd like to report an upcoming murder.*"

The recording cut out. Christopher looked horrified. "Is he reporting . . . did he know . . . ?" Eventually he landed on, "You think Lyle had something to do with what happened to Rylan?"

"I'm not counting anything out," I said, moving away from the computer in the hope it would make our conversation less forensic. "Tell me about Pearse. He had a chip on his shoulder, right?"

"How do you mean?"

I waved at the walls. "No degrees, no diplomas. Most people show off their education in their office. He's compensating for that by hiring world-renowned architects, building dazzling theaters, splashing out on expensive talent. Proving himself, perhaps, to people who looked down at him when he was younger. He was self-made, I understand. Didn't come from money?"

Christopher nodded. "Got kicked out of school in tenth grade. Yeah, if you want to read into it like that, I suppose he was trying to prove that he was a success even without an education."

"You're the counselor," I said. I traced my fingers along the trophies. Another display of his success. "Why'd he get kicked out? Anything sinister? Drugs?"

Christopher looked appalled. "No. Never. Pearse is, sorry, *was* better than us. Well, me anyway. Why would you ask that?"

"He had a needle mark in his arm," I said, choosing to leave out the bit about the bloodwork being clean.

"Not after what happened to his brother." Christopher didn't even pause to think about it. "Maybe he had some medical thing? Donated blood? It couldn't have been drugs, definitely not. The only vice Pearse had was overindulging in red wine. I've spent enough nights on his couch after a few bottles to know that."

It seemed like their friendship was genuine. "Palace like that, and Lyle doesn't have a guest bedroom?" I asked, having already seen there was a guest bedroom downstairs.

"Fancy house, shit plumbing." Christopher laughed. "Upstairs pipes rattle right through the guest room, tricky to sleep if people use the bathroom. And Erin's like clockwork. If Lyle's had a few bottles too, it's like sleeping in a ship's belly. I'll take the couch, thank you very much."

"You could always sleep in the cheese room."

"Ha. Wish his tenth-grade teachers could see that. Look, I think that's why he helped me, you know? School just didn't suit him. Couldn't keep up. Back then they'd turf you for dragging. These days they'd probably be more nuanced in their assessment, try and help. He might not have faced drugs, but Pearse knew what people expected of him, because of his lack of education." Christopher wiped his eye with the back of his hand. "He wanted to surpass that. And then when he was exposed to this population, which is also so overlooked and undersupported—I think he saw in me a similar victim of expectation."

"One last question, if you will. Did Pearse have a particular thing for Christmas?"

"Dunno," said Christopher. "Nothing more than the fact that, well, doesn't everyone like it? He's got that advent calendar, takes part in the Secret Santa. I don't even do that. I think it's weird for anyone to have to buy their counselor a present."

"Lyle rigs it so he always gets Flick anyway."

Christopher laughed. "Does he? Fair enough. Point is, I'm sure he liked Christmas."

"Most years," I said darkly, then moved to the door. "I'm going to see if I can get a glimpse of how this guillotine works. You said everyone else is downstairs with the police?"

"That's right," Christopher said. "I saw Shaun taking the cops through the guillotine earlier. He'll be in his workshop, most likely."

"Like an elf." I checked the coast was clear and then headed into the green room. "If an elf built the machine that murdered Santa."

We made our way down the stairs and ducked into the theater, scurrying quickly behind a gigantic black curtain to cross the stage. I followed Christopher down another hallway to a closed door with a *Hazardous* sign and a cartoon of safety glasses and earmuffs. Christopher rapped a knuckle on the door to no response. He turned to me. "You still got that keycard?"

I held it up to the scanner and the door whirred and unlocked. Christopher stepped back as I cracked open the door. "You really think that device killed Rylan?" he asked. "It was just a piece of paper."

"So's the Declaration of Independence. The Bible. Paper's killed more people than any blade."

"Academically, sure. But paper's still never lopped off anyone's head."

"There's a first time for everything." I pushed open the door. "That's what I'm here to find out."

19

COMIC
SANS

CHAPTER 20

The workshop reminded me of metalwork class at high school. Paint-spattered thick wooden benches were clamped with vices, mirrors, panes of glass and balsa wood were propped up everywhere, and all manner of hammers, saws and chains hung from the walls. The unfired revolver from the bullet catch trick lay on one of the benches. A lathe, a hydraulic press and a buzz-saw completed the serial killer's fantasy of a lair. At the far end of the room a roller door opened directly to the outside.

Shaun turned around as the latch clicked behind me. He was wearing thick, battered gloves covered in scorch marks, a brown leather apron and a full face shield smeared with grime. He held a soldering iron in one hand, tip still glowing; a bright red orb was clamped in a vice behind him. On a table beside that sat a notebook.

He levered up the face shield. His hair was pasted to his brow, cheeks flushed. "You lost, mate?" he said, and then recognition caught up to his tongue. "You're the guy from the show. You some kind of detective?"

That covered pretty much all bases so I said, "Yeah." I motioned behind him to his project. "Strange time to be doing work."

"I gotta wait here in case you lot think of any more questions, don't I?" Shaun rolled his eyes. "May as well keep myself busy." He picked up the object, and I saw it was Theresa's reindeer headdress from the show, antlers fixed to a headband that was in turn anchored to a strap that came down over the bridge of the nose like a Roman helmet. A red bulb for a nose completed the contraption. Shaun shook it and the nose lit up. "Motion sensor conked out. Easy fix."

"I wanted to ask you about the guillotine," I said.

"I already told you guys everything." He shook his head. "Fat lot of good it'll do. I know glazed eyes when I see them."

"I'm more interested in what you didn't tell the others. To be honest, Shaun, you're in trouble."

His shoulders tightened. "I've *been* helping you guys." It was a child's complaint, marinated in how unfair he found everything.

"I'm trying to figure out whether you really don't know, or whether you're protecting someone else. Also, how have the police, uh, I mean, *my colleagues*"—this was the first time I'd outright lied about this, but he seemed to be responding to authority—"not taken that into evidence?" I pointed at the gun.

"Did it kill anybody?" Shaun put down the soldering iron and pulled off one glove. I suppose Sullivan thought the same thing. That and checking the gun would amount to taking advice from me, an amateur. "Still got the bullet in it if you want a show. I don't know shit else."

"You built all this." I waved an arm around the workshop. "You know *some* shit." I darted forward and snatched the notebook off the bench. Shaun swatted at me, but I backed off quickly, held it aloft. I'm not particularly swift, but Shaun was slow to move in his coal-miner's getup.

"Man, give it."

I flicked through the book. It was filled with sketches and designs of various tricks. Some I'd seen at the show, others I hadn't. Some had large X's through the page. One page was missing, roughly torn out.

I stopped flicking when I got to the page with the guillotine, which also had a large X through it. Held it up for Shaun to see. "These are brilliant designs. How does it feel propping up a coke-sniffing drunk who can't even tell his wax bullets apart? These are all yours, right, the tricks that Rylan uses?"

Shaun blushed and looked at his shoes, which was the reaction I'd expected. I didn't push it.

"Now you need to tell me something. The guillotine trick has a trapdoor in the floor, right?"

"I can't tell you the magician's sec—"

"Blood, blood, blood. Everything comes down to it. A suspect covered in it. A message written in it." Shaun looked confused, because he didn't know all the clues I did, but I didn't want that to get in the way of a good monologue. "But Rylan's blood has bothered me the whole time. I just wasn't sure why. Now I think I know. *There's not enough of it*." I raised my eyebrows. "I don't care if you magicians have a vow or a code or whatnot. Just tell me: There's a trapdoor in the stage, isn't there? The blood must have siphoned through the crack in the floor."

Shaun, finally, gave an unhappy nod. He strode over to me and snatched the notebook back. Instead of scurrying off as I'd expected, he held it up and traced the sketch with his finger. "You've already seen that Rylan's back and cloak are duplicates, a shell that his real self goes into. And yes, there's a trapdoor underneath. The point of the trick is for it to go wrong. He's supposed to get his head cut off." He hesitated. "Not his real one, obviously."

"So when the timer goes off, I assume Rylan drops into the floor, his fake head rolls out, and then he reappears on the other side of the stage or something?"

"Almost. He reappears above the stage, levitates down. That is when I *lose control*," he said, leaning on the words, "of the gun, and all those cogs and stuff turn the device—we do some nonsense about it being locked to his genetic signature, that's why it was locked into the stage so it can reposition on rails. Bang. The wax bullet dissolves harmlessly into the air. Rylan spits out a pre-fired bullet casing." He sprinkled his fingers lazily, his voice flat. "Ta da. Magic. Just like murder mysteries, when you know how it works, it's all a bit . . ." He pulled a face and shrugged. "Mundane."

"How can it go wrong, then?"

"It can't . . . well, it *shouldn't*. Everything in the guillotine trick is safe. The locks are trick latches. The blade is paper. The stocks themselves have a release. Rylan could stand up and walk out of the trick at any time."

"Except you wouldn't let him," I reminded him. Rylan had gone to lift the stocks, and it was Shaun who had encouraged him to stay put. *Relax*, he'd said. *Paper, remember.*

Shaun puffed his chest. "Well, that's your fault. You told me there was a real bullet in the gun. The guillotine frame has a laser in it that, when broken, cues the next part of the trick, which is the gun moving and the firing mechanism. Normally the falling blade will split the laser, but it could also be set off by pushing the stocks up early. Turns out moving the table *was* enough so the gun didn't go off, but I didn't know that at the time. Once we moved the table away from Rylan, I thought it might be volatile. We had audience members onstage. I wanted Rylan to stay in the stocks to keep everyone *else* safe. Those bullets are Rylan's own stupid fault. I don't know why he insists on having a real one inspected by the crowd when he can't tell them apart himself. I warned him, but he wanted the element of danger."

"He got it," I said, looking around the room.

Shaun put his hands on his hips. "None of this tells me why you want to see underneath the stage."

I patted him on the back. "Like you said, once you know how it all works, magic is all a little *eh*. Obviously, whatever divorced Rylan's head from his body *wasn't* just a piece of paper. Because that's impossible. Maybe the blade didn't come from above at all. Maybe it came from below."

Shaun nodded slowly, turning it over. "You'll need a light down there."

"I've got my phone."

"It's too bright. They'll see it through the gaps in the stage." He rolled his eyes. "Come on, I know you're not a real policeman."

He handed me a light. I held it up, unimpressed.

"Really? I think this is taking the Christmas theme a bit too seriously."

CHAPTER 21

Rudolph's glowing red nose bounced against my own as we made our way under the stage. The corridor tightened as the stairs descended, finally spitting us into the bowels of the auditorium. It was several degrees colder. I could hear footsteps thudding on the floorboards above, voices trickling down. Rudolph's nose gave only a meter or so of illumination, and it tinged my vision red. Shadowy pillars bisected the darkness.

I knew immediately we were in the right spot. I was getting used to the smell of dried blood.

Above me, a sliver of rectangular light in the ceiling looked like the outline of the stage's trapdoor. I turned to point it out to Shaun, but he was no longer behind me: he'd slipped off into the darkness.

On the topic of suspects accommodating my inquiries, it occurred to me that one such reason might be to lure me somewhere alone.

I edged forward, following the thin line of brightness until I was nearly under it. A shadow flitted between the pillars to my left just as my foot crunched on something. My chest heaved as I imagined it being some piece of Rylan Blaze, some kind of bone. I crouched down.

I'd stepped on a jagged piece of glass.

This was thicker than the glass I'd found in Lyle's kitchen, half a centimeter at least. It was a large chunk too; my foot had split it down the middle. I stooped over, hoping my nose would light the way. There was glass all over the floor. It looked like someone had broken a mirror.

"It's a brilliant murder, isn't it?" whispered a voice in my ear. Shaun. I started. His face glowed red from my paltry nasal light source. He held a large triangular dagger of glass in his gloved hand, and he was turning it over, inspecting it. "Clever."

"How?" I couldn't take my eyes from the shard in his hand.

"Glass is underrated for strength. It doesn't have any *lateral* hardness, which is why we think of it as fragile, easily breakable. But along the edge, it's as strong as metal. If you mounted a piece of glass behind the paper blade, it would be basically invisible when wheeling the trick out, even if you looked at the trap from behind. Rylan is supposed to grab the bottom of the paper blade in the script, I suppose you could—"

"He cut himself." I remembered. *Tell that to my finger.* "I thought it was just a paper-cut. He must have thought the same, hence going ahead with the script. But he'd sliced his finger on the hidden glass."

Shaun nodded. "Rylan never did know his own tricks. Only here for the applause."

"So *both* blades drop, but only one, the paper, stays in the stocks. The glass one detaches and passes through Rylan, and then the gap in the stage. It'd have to be precise, but everything on a magician's stage is precise." The more I thought about it, the more I believed it. Both in person, and freeze-framed on Josh's video, the blade had seemed invisible. Not invisible though: transparent. Under the stage, with the chaos above, the killer could secretly clean up and dispose of the broken glass. The police would be looking for an actual blade. The murderer must have overesti-mated their ability to slip away, I thought, to leave this mess here.

I refocused on Shaun. "Would it be sharp enough? There's a lot of . . . *gunk* in someone's neck."

"The human body is one of the most resilient, incredible things in the natural world. It's also a squishy meat-filled bag that can cark it by laughing too hard. Yeah, I think so. Gravity does most of the work. If you're careful, you could run the glass edge along a belt sander or a lathe to sharpen it up, just to remove chance. Or you could craft it as a point-down triangle: so the point goes in the neck first." Shaun paused, then added dryly. "I am aware those tools are in my workshop. But there's no point lying about it to you, I assume."

He was right: I'd been just about to point the machinery out to him.

"Like I said." The shard in Shaun's hand gleamed. He was gazing at the broken glass and blood. He seemed, for lack of a better word, *impressed*. "Brilliant."

I'd filled my tolerance for dark spaces with potential murderers, and we fumbled our way back to the door. I couldn't help agreeing with Shaun. It *was* a brilliant murder. So brilliant that the killer didn't even have to be in the building for it to work.

Hell, they didn't even have to be *alive*.

21

INVISIBLE

To:

THERESA LIN

From:

IT'S A SECRET!

CHAPTER 22

Sam was lying on the couch scrolling through her phone when I knocked on, then opened, her sister's dressing room door. I was starting to be able to tell the twins apart, if not physically, at the very least from the disparity in confidence. I could tell the woman on the couch was the younger sibling by the way her eyes widened upon seeing me, and she scanned the room for help.

"I just want to talk a minute, Sam, if that's okay." While I'd been looking for Theresa, Sam was next on my list. I sat down next to her. She scooted away from me until her back was against the armrest, pulled her knees up and wrapped her arms around them. She gave a timid little nod. "You knew about the guillotine. You tried to tell me. I'm sorry I got it wrong."

A little head shake.

"I know you're scared." I thought back to her hissed whisper at the theater. *Not Pearse.* And how quickly she'd run off. Just like Dinesh. "If you tell me, it'll be okay."

"I already told someone," she whispered. "And look what happened."

It took a second for it to click in. I was glad I was sitting down. "Lyle?" I said. "You *told* Lyle?"

Sam's chin moved slowly up, then down.

"Told him what exac—"

"Oy!" Theresa blustered into the room. She was dressed casually: jeans and a cardigan. "You leave my sister alone, she's been through enough." I stood up and Theresa took my seat, put a hand on her sister's knee. She stared daggers at me. "Haven't you had your fill yet?"

I tried not to let my annoyance show. Twice now, Sam had been on the verge of telling me something, and twice she'd been scared off. I could tell by the way she looked at Theresa that Sam wouldn't say anything more without her sister's approval. "I'm just trying to help."

"Well, going over the same old trauma isn't going to help anyone." Theresa stood up and guided me into the corridor. "Look at her, she can't take much more of this. You know how close she is to relapsing? Undoing all her hard work?" I realized she was pleading with me. "Can't you just, you know, leave her out of this bit?"

"You're worried she might—" My eyes flicked down to the scar on the inside of her wrist. Theresa, heralded as speeding through the program so much faster than her sister, wasn't without her own demons.

Theresa pulled her sleeve down. "That's not what it looks like. When I was younger, I needed some extra money." She sighed, realizing she'd have to explain. "Every junkie's done a break-in somewhere. We all know how sharp glass can be. That's my point: this . . . this . . . *devil* pushes you to the edge. Don't take Samantha there."

"I'm only looking for the truth," I said, which sounded like something a real detective would say.

"Here's some truth. I would do anything to protect my sister." She reached out and grabbed my arm. Her grip was firm. I could feel five fingertip-sized bruises forming. Her gaze was hypnotic. "*Anything*. So think about that before you bring her into this."

I convinced Theresa to give me back my arm, and to join me for a cup of tea, by promising not to accuse her sister of anything further. We headed upstairs to the kitchenette off the green room. The mound of presents under the tree failed, at this point, to inject me with any Christmas spirit. While the tea bags were steeping, I asked her what I'd originally planned to, when I'd opened her dressing room door and found Sam instead: "Does hypnotism work?"

She seemed surprised by the question. "Mr. Fair Play Mystery— yes, I've read your books—wants to know if hypnotism's real? I thought you weren't allowed any *clues of the divine*." She made air quotes around the last phrase.

"I figure your act is as much psychology as it is supernatural, so it's fair play enough for me. That's why I'm asking: Does it work?"

"Do you believe in magic?"

"No."

"Then not on you." She shrugged. "You have to be suggestible."

"I'm highly suggestible," I suggested.

"I'm sure you are." She blew steam off the top of her cup and handed me the other. "But not for hypnotism."

"You ever hypnotized your sister?"

Thereas shook her head. "I wouldn't do that. The audience gives consent, you know."

"For those who are susceptible . . ." I took a scalding sip and replayed the show in my mind: Theresa clicking her fingers and her volunteers coming to their senses, returning to their seats clueless to the embarrassments she'd just put them through. "Can it really make you forget things?"

She sucked her teeth. "Not forget. Not really. It's still there in your brain, but yeah, I suppose I cover it up more than delete it. Bob from Accounts doing a Chicken Dance in his underpants wouldn't be as funny if he remembered it." She winked at me. "That's obviously not the family-friendly show."

"Would Rylan have known hypnotism?"

She shrugged. "Most magicians probably know the principles. Whether or not they can pull it off is another question."

"It's a unique path. How'd you come to be interested in this as a job, anyway?"

"You know they use it to quit smoking, right? Well, the Pearse Foundation used it back in the day to help us manage withdrawals. Not anymore, it's an outdated technique. I found it fascinating though, decided to study it. I've been working clubs, festivals, with my act for a while. But when the foundation announced Rylan as the tour for this year, I thought it was a good chance to take it on the road. I asked Lyle if I could be the support act."

"And to look after Sam." It wasn't a question.

"Rumor had it Rylan loved a little glass of Nosé." She tapped her nose. "Celebrity trumps irony, I think, in terms of how much money Flick wants to make. Sorry, *raise*." She rolled her eyes. "That's like hiring a bear to guard honey."

I'd heard Pearse's voice memo: *If I see him with a substance around my graduates again.* "Pearse had concerns . . ." I left it hanging, dangling the carrot.

Theresa was, as it happens, hungry. "Sam tries, okay? She's just, well, easily tempted. I don't think she took anything. I mean, she told me she didn't. And she's pretty good like that, with me anyway." She seemed a little self-righteous. I'd bet she had a mug with *World's Best Sister* on it, possibly the receipt as well. "I'm glad it was as clear to Lyle as it was to me that Rylan was getting in the way."

"In the way?"

"Of her recovery." She rolled her eyes. "God, stop salivating: it's not a confession."

"You and Lyle are both alike, I think." The corner of her mouth twitched, even though I hadn't implied a compliment yet. "You both stand up for the little guy. Right?"

"Absolutely." She seemed pleased. "When I found out Rylan had offered my sister cocaine, I had it out with him. Absolutely lost it. Told him I'd—" She cleared her throat, realized she was off course, and tapered off her sentence.

"Kill him?"

"Something like that." Her voice had switched to warm and soothing, like honey. Like the one she used onstage. I wondered just how suggestible I was. I wouldn't be much of a detective if someone could confess to a murder and then click their fingers and I forgot all about it. Maybe they already had. This might be the second or even third or fourth time I was investigating these murders.

"You're being awfully candid for a murder suspect," I said. "Everyone is, actually."

"That's because you can pluck around our motives all you like, but we didn't do anything. Sam especially, and I know that for a fact."

"For a fact," I echoed. "Does she have an alibi you haven't told me?"

Her eyes narrowed. "Why single us out? Because you think my sister is weak? She's not weak because she relapses. The fact she's not fallen off a hundred more wagons, the fact she's still going, makes her the strongest woman I know. Stronger than you."

"She is," I agreed. "And she wants to do what's right. But I'm stuck. How did she know something was going to happen to Rylan? How did Dinesh? Did you?"

Theresa chuckled. "Isn't that how your mysteries work? Everyone's got a motive. Everyone's got a secret?"

"Everyone's got two secrets, actually." I tried to lighten the mood, nodding at the Christmas tree. "If you include the Secret Sant—"

My mouth suddenly forgot how to make sounds. My jaw locked. The presents.

I ran over to the tree, practically sliding on my knees like a soccer player after slotting a goal, and grabbed the big blue box with the tag: *To: Rylan Blaze, From: KK.* It was easily the biggest present in the bunch. But it was also, I realized as I grabbed it, the lightest.

I tore back the shiny blue wrapping, then used my keys to knife open the box.

It was empty.

Some detectives, perhaps, solve crimes like fireworks: one lit fuse exploding everything at once. I solve crimes like a ten-car rear-ender on a bumper-to-bumper freeway: one car slams into another, and another and another, all the way up the line.

The box was empty.

Smash.

Because why bother buying a present for a dead man?

Smash-Smash-Smash.

I looked up at Theresa. "I just solved a murder."

"*A murder?*" She stood up rod straight. "Just one?"

"Yeah."

"Which one?"

I stood up. "One that never happened."

22

DEAD MAN'S
PRESENT

CHAPTER 23

We're back to where we started. Erin.

She sat across from me in the same holding cell. Her cheeks were slightly less ruddy, eyelids relieved of tearful rubbing, and forensics had at last let her wash her hands and hair. It would be a cliché to say she looked thinner, as a more accurate description would be that there was *less of her*. It wasn't so much a physical loss. It was the glassiness in her eyes. She took up less space in the room.

The station wasn't taking visitors by the time I'd scurried out of the theater, so I'd had to wait until the next morning to be admitted. This had given me another sweat-drenched evening turning things over in my head. I'd solved one hypothetical murder, which had possibly tailgated and run up the back of the other two (the ones that actually happened) but all I had was supposition. In a legal sense, I had absolutely nothing. Just a woman covered in her boyfriend's blood, with no memory of how it happened. I was still waiting for my lightbulb moment.

"I do have a theory," I said, after I'd filled Erin in on the empty box and everything I'd seen. "Which I've already shared with Sullivan." I tilted my head at the cell bars. "He obviously isn't buying it, otherwise you'd be on the other side of these." I let out a huge sneeze across the table between us, wiped my nose. "Don't get your hopes up. Without anything firm, it's just a theory."

Erin grabbed a tissue and wiped the table where I'd sneezed. The shiny aluminum squeaked under her rubbing. And yes, before you think it, that was a part of my newly advanced interrogation techniques.

"I'll take theories," she said. "Hit me."

"What if Rylan Blaze and Lyle Pearse killed each other?"

"You don't remember if Lyle was in the bed next to you when you got up to use the bathroom," I explained. So it's possible he went out to the theater, and spent the night rigging the glass guillotine. That would explain why he'd opened his advent calendar on the day he died. I guess he could have nicked his finger on the glass, which is where the droplets of blood on your bathroom wall might have come from, once he'd gotten home and washed his hands." Erin's eyes tilted up, imagining Lyle slicing his finger, shaking his injured hand back and forth in pain. A small cut could have easily reopened hours later. "That's why he had the page from Shaun's notebook, he was studying the mechanics of the tricks."

Erin was nodding slowly. I could see her adding up everything I was saying against the clues I'd told her previously. Her face quivered, unable to settle on an emotion: the excitement of freedom was being doused by the horror that Lyle himself could be a murderer.

I pushed on. "Rylan figures out that Lyle is planning to execute him. Perhaps he stays late at the theater and busts him mid-prep, follows him home. Perhaps they arrange to meet: to discuss the sale of the foundation's assets. That I can only guess at. So Rylan arrives at your and Lyle's house. Now, depending on my guess from before, he either follows Lyle in, or Lyle is waiting for him. Rylan knows that Lyle is planning to kill him, he just doesn't know it's in motion already, so he thinks he has to strike first. Rylan kills Lyle with a knife from your knife block. He sets up the scene to frame you—"

Erin's forehead crinkled with concern. "How?"

"Um, well, he's very skilled at sleight of hand," I offered weakly. "My guess is that card tricks and the like need a delicate touch, delicate enough that you don't wake up while he puts blood on you. And you've got your headphones blaring Tokyo traffic or whatever. Even if you woke up, he is a magician who possibly has some knowledge of hypnotism. So Rylan sets up the scene to incriminate you, and he thinks he's home free, completely unaware that Lyle's booby trap is ready for him the following night. And you know everything from there."

Erin weighed me up. Her oscillating emotions had landed, disappointingly, on confusion. "Motives?"

"Aside from getting ahead of Lyle's plan to kill *him*, Rylan wanted to buy the Pearse Foundation, but Lyle was holding out. As for Lyle, Rylan was offering cocaine to his graduates, particularly Sam. Lyle was livid. And he was fragile after firing Dinesh, someone whose success he was proud of, who encapsulated what the foundation stood to achieve. My guess is Lyle narrowed the cracks in the foundation to one bad seed: Rylan."

Erin was shaking her head. "This isn't like you, Ern. I count five guesses. You don't guess. You tie up every little piece. That's what you do. Whose murder did Lyle call in? Rylan's, or his own?"

"I guess—"

"Six."

I put my head in my hands. There were, admittedly, a few holes. I hadn't even come close to linking the bloodied message *Christmas* or the needle mark in Lyle's arm, let alone Rylan's empty present. But it was the best I could do. What I did know didn't fit together yet. Not to mention my whole timeline depends on chocolate consumption.

"You want me to be innocent," Erin said. I looked up at her.

She was staring at her hands, and I could see she was picturing bloody spots on them. "But I don't need your faith. I want the truth. Even if the truth of it is"—she held up her palms—"what these hands can do. I'll own what—"

I raised my own hand and clicked my fingers in front of her forehead. The single loud, clean snap echoed off the cell walls.

There was a beat of awkward silence.

"What was that about?" Erin said. "Is this another one of your bizarre interrogation techniques?"

"Worth a shot," I grumbled.

I know. I know. Pretty flimsy mystery if a hypnotic mind wipe was at its center. I was annoyed at myself for trying it. But I was desperate.

"Listen." I leaned forward. "I only have half a theory about Rylan's murder. And I can't figure how you and Lyle fit in. I know you're innocent, I just don't know how. The way to get you out is to pin it on two dead men who set out to destroy each other. For our purposes, this theory will work."

"And the real killer gets away?" Erin reached out and touched my cheek. "That's not you either."

I'm supposed to be a reliable narrator, and here I am caught lying to myself. Does that mean I do have a nemesis after all? An arch-enemy doesn't need a body count or a master plan, they simply make the detective *change*. I'd compromised myself, so I'd lost.

"You know, it's stupid," Erin said, then laughed sadly. "I'm still sitting here, hoping you'll figure it all out. The way you did on the mountain. The way I read it happened on the train. What do you call it in your books? I really wished for that moment."

"Me too." I could barely get it out. My eyes were hot. Wet. "It's called a lightbulb moment."

Then I froze. The freeway piled up.

"I just had one," I whispered.

"What?"

I exploded into, on reflection, near-maniacal laughter. I stood up, merely to burn energy. "I just had *a lightbulb moment*!" I was talking quickly, thoughts like shotgun pellets. "Lyle never left your house that night. He wouldn't have had time to rig the guillotine by the time you . . . and he would have had to already be dead . . ." I pointed at Erin. "I know how you got blood on you."

A knock at the door. "You okay in there?"

"Yeah, we're, um," Erin called, examining me, "fine?"

I sat down and put my hands on both her shoulders. "I need to ask you one more question about Lyle. If you answer how I think you will, I might be about to catch a killer."

I am going to go against the principles of fair play mysteries here and hide from you the question I asked Erin. Just for a couple of pages, I promise. Besides, you've got all the clues to figure it out yourself, so I'm not actually hiding anything. I'm just taking away the training wheels.

I asked her the question as the guard opened the door.

"Yeah," Erin said instantly, confused. "He had his processes. It flared up when he was stressed."

She must have seen my smile almost split my skull open. I was out of the seat and into the corridors before she could blink. Only her curious voice followed me.

"How the hell is *that* supposed to keep me out of jail?"

23

**LIGHTBULB
MOMENT**

LIFE'S NOT FAIR

No door to open on this section, I'm afraid. Like Andy says, they can't all be chocolates.

I've solved it. But, like every good Christmas lunch, final preparations must be made. I spent the rest of the twenty-third sliding six letters under the doors of the dressing rooms at the theater. All of them said: *And for my final trick*. Below that was an address and a time of 8 a.m., December 24. I emailed our favorite journalist too. I was sure he'd want the exclusive.

I was getting quite good at sneaking around police officers, though the number of them had dwindled at the theater. No one noticed me leave the envelopes, same as no one noticed me leave Shaun's workshop with something wrapped in my coat.

Mysteries are a team sport, I always hold to that. Except for my minor transgression in the last chapter, you have all twenty-three pieces to find out what's behind door number twenty-four. You should have everything you need to, excuse the pun, take a stab at it.

So here we are. The final door.

CHAPTER 24

After three days at roasting, the town was overcooked. The colors were bleached out of the fallen wildflower petals. My shoes crunched over every desiccated leaf and shred of grass as I made my way to the Cable Car station at Echo Point, conscious of the specific weight in my backpack clunking against my spine. The sign out the front of the station said *Closed: December 24– December 26, New Year's Day*. The Cable Car itself was in the dock. A giant turnstile sat above it, from which a taut, thick wire stretched out over the misty valley.

I was fifteen minutes early, but Shaun and Flick had beaten me there. After sincere and hushed greetings, we stood in knowing silence. Flick tapped away at her phone.

Christopher was the next to show up. He shook my hand and patted me on the back.

Josh Felman arrived next. "On the record?" he said, fiddling with various dials across his vest and a sound-mixing app on his iPhone.

Dinesh gave me an embarrassed little wave as he sauntered up the steps. At 8:05, just as I was starting to worry that maybe my psychological gamble—that the innocent would come to be proved so, and the guilty would come because it would make them look more guilty not to—was misguided, a cab pulled up and discharged Sam and Theresa. Sam looked at her shoes the whole walk up the path, while Theresa pierced me with that very same look she'd given me previously: *don't mess with my sister*. I was banking on that attitude, actually. My life kind of depended on it.

"What are we doing here?" Shaun said, at last. There was a murmur of relief that he'd broken the seal for everyone.

"You'll see," I said, as a man in a blue boiler suit emerged from the control booth and unclipped the rope in front of the Cable Car. The doors opened like an elevator's and I guided everyone inside. The cabin was large enough for all of us and then some, but everything feels claustrophobic when a killer's involved. Everyone stood, ignoring the seats around the walls.

I don't possess Josh's knack for bribery. Luckily, the operator didn't want for concert tickets or flight upgrades. Two cases of beer and a hundred-dollar bill was motivation enough.

"You all got my note," I said, at which there was a hum of nervousness. "Our friend in the booth here has agreed to take us back and forth across the valley a couple of times so that we have the required privacy."

"And so none of us can run," Flick offered, a lilt of annoyance in her voice.

"Exactly. At each dock, I'm going to let off those I've deduced to be innocent, until we whittle it down to the final culprit or culprits. Yes, it's a little theatrical. But, I'm sure you'll agree, fitting."

The floor underneath us jolted as the Cable Car started moving. Sam and Shaun reached out for the rail that ran above our heads. The Cable Car had a glass bottom, and the cliffside dropped away beneath our feet.

"Where to start? Six of the seven of you wanted to kill Rylan Blaze. Two of you tried. And one of you succeeded."

"Every one of you has motive." I figured I'd start at the top of the organization, and so turned to the interim head. "Flick."

She seemed annoyed to be first chosen. "Get it out of the way," she said, as if she was running late to a meeting. Which, to be fair, was her usual tone.

"I considered that you might have killed Lyle to get the position of interim head of the Pearse Foundation. I understand you were even less willing to sell than Lyle was, especially when Lyle started coming around to the offer. So it's possible that you killed Lyle first, and Rylan found out about it, and so he had to go too. But I kept getting stuck on the selling. You'd have gotten very nice dividends. *Why* didn't you want to sell?"

"*Not* taking the money is hardly motive," Flick scoffed.

"We'll get there. Sam," I pivoted. We were now halfway across the canyon. The vertigo was dizzying if you looked down. A hawk flew underneath us. "Blaze was dangerous for your recovery. And Theresa, you'd do anything to protect your little sister. You told me Rylan was *in the way*."

Theresa's eyes were fire. Sam still looked at the floor.

"Dinesh, you believe Rylan got you fired. You swear you didn't take the ring, which, if you're telling the truth, means that someone put it in your bag to get you fired. Rylan cost you your job, and Lyle's trust."

"I can't deny the motive, but I do deny everything else," Dinesh said.

I nodded. "Lucky for you, you get a second shot at the person who ruined your life."

Dinesh's brow crinkled but it was Shaun who spoke up. "Are you saying Rylan is still—"

"Rylan's dead alright," I said. "He's not that good a magician. But he's not the one who got Dinesh fired. Flick, you did that."

Dinesh clenched his jaw so tight I thought he'd crack a tooth. He spun to Flick. Though he was too far away to lash out, she put her hands out in defense.

"I can explain," she stuttered.

"You'd better," Dinesh growled.

"I'll handle that actually," I cut in. "It's kind of my job. Flick, Rylan told me that Lyle was overvaluing the company by half a million dollars. He said his guy couldn't match up the outgoing expenses. Being that you were the CFO, I assume Rylan's team brought it to you. He didn't suspect you, perhaps he simply thought it was a minor accounting error of no consequence, so he didn't even know what he was doing. You realized you were about to get caught: you've been embezzling hundreds of thousands of dollars from the charity. You have expensive taste. I may not know Mortgart, but I know McQueen, who you told me you were wearing at the show."

Now the rest of the car turned to Flick. Expressions varied from disgust (Sam and Shaun) to outright murderous (Dinesh, Christopher and Theresa). And, of course, excited (Josh).

"You had to shift the blame," I explained directly to Flick. "You planted the ring in Dinesh's bag, and then told Lyle he'd stolen it. Both Rylan and Lyle knew the meeting you called was to deal with a *theft*. They just thought Dinesh had stolen different things. Lyle thought he was dealing with a property theft, Rylan thought it was patching the hole in the finances. It was a risky plan, revolving around Dinesh's short fuse cutting off the conversation, which you told me about when you first showed me a picture of him, and your advice to Lyle to *rip the bandage off quickly* and make sure he had the first word. All you had was a Hail Mary, and it worked. Dinesh lost his cool and started throwing trophies before he got to defend himself against accusations he didn't even understand."

Dinesh had told me this, in the dark bushland: *I didn't even know what I was accused of stealing.*

"Flick told you, Dinesh, about the ring later, while she helped you pack your things." I turned back to Flick. "That's your motive for murder. I thought from the start it was strange you gave me so much access to the business. I was an amateur, I wasn't going to get as forensic as the police, especially not on the accounting. You said you wanted a fast resolution, minimal reputational damage. I told you I only did the opposite. Turns out that was what you wanted: the company's reputation tarnished enough that the investors back off. Selling the company would have entailed a more detailed audit. You'd have certainly been caught then. And that's why you couldn't sell."

I addressed the entire room again. "Let's dig deeper. Dinesh's termination was the start of Lyle's crisis of faith, the first crack in his belief in his work. That crack would widen, eroding his trust in those around him, and lead to the decision to sell the company, and, eventually, his death."

Josh spoke up. "So when he decided to sell the foundation, Flick killed him?"

I shrugged. "Without proof it's just motive. I haven't finished yet. Shaun"—Shaun opened his arms wide as I turned to him, as if to say *bring it on*—"you've been playing second fiddle to Blaze all this time. Your designs, your builds, made him famous. Made him rich. Blaze doesn't even know which bullet in his showstopper is wax. Meanwhile, you're still scrubbing bird poo off his shoes. It's not hard to imagine why you were fantasizing about offing Blaze. You're the talent in the act, reduced to playing second fiddle. And Rylan gets all the glory, all the *riches*. From *your* tricks. That must hurt."

Shaun leaned against a side window, which made the whole car rock on its wires. Sam's knuckles went white against her handhold. "So what? Who hasn't thought about offing their boss? It's *not a crime*. Otherwise half the country'd be in jail. I made the guy what he is and got squat in return. I'm entitled to my imagination."

Everyone eyed each other up. We were almost at the other side.

"You can't stop us getting out," Christopher said, blowing his wisp of hair out of his face. This was greeted by a chorus of agreement. "I'm not particularly comfortable being trapped in a floating box with a murderer."

"I can't stop you, no. But don't you want to know who's guilty?" I scanned the carriage. "And doesn't the guilty party want to find out just how much I know?"

This quietened the objections to a grumble.

"It's all a bit"—Josh spun a finger in the air—"circumstantial. Isn't it?"

"It is. Let's stick to the facts instead. Josh, what year did you graduate from the foundation?"

Accusing suspects in a room—be it, in my experience, a library, a bar in a train, or a Cable Car almost three hundred meters above the treetops—is like watching a tennis match. People's heads swivel left and right depending on the accusation. Now everyone swiveled to Josh Felman.

He was, of course, the journalist with his back to the photographer in the framed picture in Pearse's office.

"You trash me in the papers every chance you get. And then you follow me out here and simply hand over crucial, and illegal, documents that relate to the case? Medical reports, police files. I never believed that you just wanted the story. Plus you got into the sold-out gala. Which means you knew someone well enough to call in a favor." We ground to a shuddering stop inside the docking station. "You don't care about Rylan's murder, but you wanted me to solve Pearse's. You felt you owed him that, didn't you?"

"He saved my life." Josh mumbled the familiar phrase.

"Same as almost everyone else here. But that didn't stop some-one killing him." I hit the button and the door slid open. "But it wasn't you. You shared information with me because you wanted the murderer caught. So get out."

And then there were six.

We left Josh, fists curled and fuming like a child too short for a carnival ride, in the dock. I spotted a few eyes looking wistfully at the exit, but no one wanted to brand themselves afraid, and so everyone stood still while the Cable Car eased back over the clifftops.

"Now we're into the good stuff," I said. "Five of you have mo-tives to kill Blaze, like I said before. What I didn't say was: all of you planned it together."

Sam started to cry.

"That's insane," Theresa erupted. "Even with your logic, my sister and I have nothing against Lyle. Shaun either. Your ex-wife has literal blood on her hands, and you stand here and accuse us?"

"I'll get to Lyle," I promised. "Five of you all decided that Rylan was toxic and had to be removed. Well, four of you, Theresa, Sam, Dinesh and Shaun, and one wanted to hide their embezzlement. Maybe it started as a dark joke. Maybe you brainstormed how to get him fired, and it transformed to this. Maybe one of you brought it to the table as a laugh before it spun out of control. It doesn't matter. The point is that the five of you got together and came up with a plan. And Shaun, you sketched out how to do it. Lyle had the bullet trick design in his desk drawer, torn from your notebook."

"Blaze didn't get done in by a bullet, he got his bloody head chopped off," Shaun said, smug.

"I didn't say you planned to use the guillotine. You'd thought about it, but you couldn't get the device right, you couldn't figure out how to get rid of the blade to make it look properly like an accident. When we were underneath the stage, you were so impressed someone figured out your conundrum by using glass. It's ironic, isn't it? Someone's been stealing your tricks for years, and now someone's stolen your murder."

"I didn't—" Shaun started.

"Just like every trick you couldn't make lethal, you crossed it out, and went with a different method. You'd thought through, and ruled out, plenty of tricks, hence all the crosses in your notebook. These sketches were more than daydreams. Your notebook isn't full of tricks, it's full of weapons."

I swiveled my backpack around to my front, unzipped it, and pulled out the revolver I'd stolen from the theater. "Eventually you landed on this. You really were going to switch the bullets." I placed the gun on the floor. "Lyle had the schematics, not for a trick but for a *murder*, in his desk drawer. Which means he knew about your plan. That's what he meant when he said he'd seen the *rotten core*. All his charges. All his friends. Murderers. So he finally agreed to sell. And he called the police to report a murder that hadn't happened yet.

"But here's the really clever part. Out of the five of you, you had to choose a killer. But should there be an investigation, you all needed to be convincing in believing it was an accident. The only way to do that was for no one to know who had done it except the person chosen. A hidden ballot. And how do you do that? It's easy. Most offices draw names out of a hat around this time of year. You used the Secret Santa."

"Spot on," Flick confirmed, clearing her throat. "It's funny, I don't remember how we got from an after-work drinks session to murder, I honestly couldn't tell you who brought it up, but one minute we're laughing about one of his tricks blowing him up onstage, the next we're planning it out. Once we'd agreed on the bullet trick, we drew our Secret Santas. Whoever pulled Rylan's name had to kill him."

"Shut up!" Theresa yelled.

Flick was grinning now. "I had *you*, Theresa. I didn't draw Blaze, so I don't care if Ernest knows the whole plan. I'm in the clear."

"If by *the clear* you mean financial fraud and conspiracy to commit murder, then yeah, you're clear," I said. "It doesn't matter who pulled the trigger if you all planned it. It's still a crime."

"But no one pulled the trigger?" Dinesh said slowly. "The bullets don't matter."

"You're ahead of me. Let's get back to the mechanics. It's a brilliant plan. Lyle can't mess it up by drawing Rylan because he rigs it every year. Each of you only knows your own draw. For everyone except the killer, every other one of you is still a valid suspect. It gives you all deniability. Like *Strangers on a Train* with a twist: you can't incriminate any one person if you don't know who it is. It's also the same principle that used to be implemented in firing squad executions: multiple rifles would fire, but only one would be loaded with a real bullet so that no single executioner would have to live with the guilt of firing the fatal shot. Of course, your murderer does know. But the rest of you equally suspect one another, which makes the case pretty much unsolvable. You're Schrödinger's murderers: simultaneously innocent and guilty." Everyone swapped glances. "If you're wondering how I figured this out, it's because whoever did draw Rylan's name wrapped an empty box for the Secret Santa. Not giving him a present would have given it away, so they had to put something under the tree.

But why buy a present for someone you knew would be dead before they opened it?"

I will never get tired of the moment the accused realizes precisely where they've gone wrong. It's a thinning of the lips, a tightening of the neck. It comes a millisecond before the realization of the larger group, because while everyone else is having the past *explained* to them, this person *remembers* it. I could see it in her face. Yes: I wrote her.

"The bullets *were* swapped," I continued. "Only one of you, the would-be killer, knew who'd pulled Rylan's name out of the hat, but the rest of you expected that person had acted. Your actions on the night showed you knew too much. Sam tried to have me intervene. At the moment of crisis onstage, Shaun wouldn't let anyone touch the gun, because he expected it to be loaded with a live round." He'd also been incredulous I'd been allowed backstage: *Flick invited you? Tonight?* "Theresa, you wouldn't let Sam stand in front of the gun for the same reason. And Dinesh, you told me yourself on the clifftop." *How'd you know about the bullets?* He'd said *know*, even though the gun hadn't fired and, at that point, to a spectator my deductions would have looked completely wrong.

I pointed at the gun. "This hasn't been touched since the show. If I'm right, that means there's still a real bullet in here. If anybody wants to shoot me: go for it. But it'll be as good as a confession."

"Bet it's empty," Theresa said. "Some trick."

"It's a prop gun, not a real one," Shaun said. "It still fires, but it only opens once fired or you need a key to access the chamber, which Ernest wouldn't have. It *could* still have the show's bullet in it."

The suspect tennis continued. Advantage detective. Everyone eyed the gun and each other.

"I think I know who drew Rylan from the Secret Santa," I said, as we pulled into the dock again. I opened the door. "Flick, Dinesh, Shaun: get off."

With three suspects left, we headed over the void for the third time. The sun was higher now and inside the glass walls of the Cable Car it felt superheated.

"I don't even *do* the Secret Santa," Christopher complained.

"Sam." I ignored him and turned to her. She was staring out the window, stubbornly refusing to acknowledge me. "I think you drew the short straw, so to speak."

Theresa stepped toward me. "Don't you dare accuse—" She glanced at the gun. My heart hung high in my chest while I waited to see if she'd pick it up.

Suddenly Sam darted across the cabin, placing herself between her sister and me. The whole carriage swayed with the movement. The treetops below blurred. "Give it up, Tee!" Sam locked eyes with me. "Yes. Okay! I admit it. It was my job to kill Blaze. The bullets are supposed to be on the table in a specific order. I switched them backstage." Her chest crumpled with the relief of confession. That glimmer of tight-necked realization that gave her away when I'd recounted her wrapping the empty box loosened.

I'd, of course, seen this in the corridor before the show. Sam begging her sister to swap Secret Santas: *It's not fair. Please swap.* And I now understood Theresa's particularly bristling response: *Don't tell me who you've got, Sam! Geez! . . . That's the whole point of the thing.* Sam hadn't wanted to do it. But she had. And then she'd regretted it, and tried to get me to stop it. *Not Pearse.*

"Despite what she said, Flick was actually the one who started the idea," Sam explained, her tongue looser now. "It was like you said. Trading stupid dark wishes about accidents. It's all *what if* and laughter. Then someone says *but seriously*, and . . . well, you know the rest. Shaun came up with the idea of making it look like a trick gone awry, he had all these ideas in his notebook. Dinesh came up with the Secret Santa thing. Everyone had a part. But I'm not shifting the blame. We *all* agreed." She looked back to the cliffside, where Flick, Dinesh and Shaun watched on, then turned to Theresa, who was shaking her head. "I'm sorry, sis, but he already knows."

"You don't even know what you're confessing to," Theresa said, through her teeth.

Sam turned back to me. "How bad is my luck to draw Rylan, right? But I couldn't let everyone down. I had to do my part. I only messed with the bullets though. I didn't tamper with the guillotine. I swear."

We were pulling up to the adjacent cliff. Fifty or so meters to go. Once I'd figured out that Sam had swapped the bullets, I knew she wasn't the killer, even though she'd intended to be.

"I know you didn't," I said. "But drawing the Secret Santa caused you a lot of anguish. The responsibility of a murder was too much. You didn't outright say that to your sister, but you begged her to swap. Which was enough for her to catch on that you'd drawn the short straw. And you know she'd do anything to protect you."

"No." Now it was Sam's turn to protect her sister. Her voice was as cold and hard and confident as I'd ever heard it. The car shuddered into the dock for one final disembarkation. We all swayed. The gun slid a few centimeters in Theresa's direction. "What are you implying?"

"After you'd made the switch, Sam, you regretted it," I said. "You tried to tell me so that I'd stop the show. When that failed, you stood in front of the bullet yourself. These aren't the actions of someone planning to go through with a murder. But those were last resorts. You'd tried to get out of the whole thing already. Four days ago, you told someone you trusted." Her whisper, in Theresa's dressing room, came back to me: *I already told someone . . . and look what happened.* "That's why Lyle had the drawing."

Theresa's eyes widened. "You told *Lyle*?"

"I had to." Sam wiped away snot. "We weren't in our right minds. I was helping us all not make a huge mistake. And look what happened to Lyle! One of the others killed him as a warning to me that I couldn't back out or speak up. That's why I went through with it." Her fear at the theater made sense now. Dinesh fleeing too. When I'd asked him who he was afraid of: *I don't know. But that's the whole point.* The plan had gone haywire, extra bodies and ruined plans, and no one knew who the killer was supposed to be. Sam believed someone was holding her, penalty of death, to the plan. Perhaps they all did.

"Pearse wasn't killed to threaten you," I said, as we arrived in the dock. "He was killed to save you."

At this, Christopher rubbed both his temples, muttered *"Unbelievable,"* picked up the gun, and pointed it squarely at my chest.

"Sam, Theresa, time for you to hop off," I said, not taking my eyes from the barrel.

They moved slowly and obediently, stunned. Then I shut the door, and a murderer and I sailed out over the gorge one last time.

24

CHRISTOPHER
SLEET

CHAPTER 25

The gun shook in Christopher's hand. Despite two murders, he hadn't developed a knack for it.

"Why are you making me do this?" he shouted. His voice echoed off the glass walls.

"I don't have any hard proof," I said. "Just deductions. But an innocent woman sits in jail for your crimes, and if taking a bullet is what it takes to get her out, then I'm prepared to do that."

"Guesswork?" Christopher spat. "You did all this off guesswork?"

"Deductions," I corrected. "But I was confident. Lyle Pearse wrote that you were the killer on his kitchen floor, after all."

"That's not *evidence*. He wrote the word *Christmas*."

"Lyle was dyslexic," I explained. This was the very last thing I'd asked Erin in the police station. Her answer: *He had his processes. It flared up when he was stressed*. "He was kicked out of school for what would now be seen as a learning disability that needs extra support. He's got no diplomas or degrees on his walls, because after he left school he wasn't well looked after by traditional education systems. He listens to audiobooks, and he's set up his office to cater best to his brain. That includes dictation software, and using Comic Sans as his default font. Sans serif fonts are easier for people with dyslexia to read, and Comic Sans, joke of the typography world as it is, is actually one of the best. Pearse hadn't forgotten to take the advent chocolate on the twelfth, nor was he in the office in the early hours of the twenty-first. Firing Dinesh on the twelfth had stressed him out, and he misread the doors. Twelve and twenty-one are the *only* numbers on an advent calendar that are reversible."

"What does that have to do with me?" Christopher sniffed.

And here it is: the true meaning of the word *Christmas*. I told you that's an important part of any Holiday Special.

"I saw a shopping list on Lyle's fridge for bread *plus* milk. People have their tics in how they write, and a plus sign was one of Pearse's: he preferred it to an ampersand. I thought from my first glimpse that the *t* in his final bloody message was short and stumpy. That's because it's not a *t* at all. It's a plus sign. He was writing Chris *plus* Sam. But his dyslexia flares up when he's stressed and I'd say dying is pretty stressful: *Sam* got jumbled, and turned into mas. He put her name because she'd confessed to him. He called the police. Then he called you for advice, and you came over. When you stabbed him, his final thought was that you were in it together, and you were protecting her. *Chris + Sam*."

"You've got nothing." Christopher looked at the gun in his hand. "And my picking this up doesn't prove anything."

I tensed, ready to move. The gun wasn't pointed at me any-more, but if he fired it could still ricochet and hit me. Or, worse, the glass floor.

"Well, not nothing," I said. "I never told you about the bloody word on the floor. You had to have seen it for yourself." We were only a third of the way across the canyon. "Lyle trusted you. He let you into his home. You went there wanting to discuss how to save the graduates from the mistake they were about to make, but you discovered that it wasn't a discussion at all. Lyle has already called the police. He wants to turn them all in and reveal the whole plan, and not only that, he's throwing in the towel on the whole foundation. Because he's seen the *rotten core*. He doesn't think people can be fixed anymore. How did that feel to you?" I pictured Christopher, who'd worked so hard to pull himself out of hell, listening to his once close friend tell him people could never change. "Was that when you grabbed the knife?"

Christopher was silent.

"Afterward, you'd realized what you'd done, and you needed to figure out how to shift the attention to Erin, asleep upstairs. This is when it gets really interesting. I found a small, thin piece of glass in that kitchen. You'd left the body sprawled because you wanted an incriminating crime scene, you left the word *Christmas*, thinking it was meaningless, and yet you went to the trouble of cleaning up a shattered glass. Why? Unless you thought those glass shards were the thing that would get you caught."

"This is *nonsense*," Christopher said. But the gun had stopped flailing, and returned to my chest.

"The glass was from a lightbulb. One that you removed from Pearse's ensuite. That was how you framed Erin. Erin's told me multiple times how traumatized she is by the serial killer that targeted our family. She tells me she still thinks about dead bodies, that she's always washing her hands. She's turned into an outright germaphobe. I sneezed in front of her just to test it, and she lasted all of five seconds before having to wipe the table. Which makes it even more strange that she doesn't have *any soap* in her bathroom. Especially when her only statement, one that makes her look guilty, is consistent with one fact: she went to the bathroom, and then she *washed her hands*."

Christopher swallowed heavily.

"Lyle's blood is clean. No sedative, and definitely no drugs. So why does he have a needle mark in his arm? After he was dead, you snuck upstairs and took the lightbulb and the soap bottle from the ensuite. Erin didn't hear you because she listens to traffic white noise while she sleeps. But she would wake up if you touched her, so you needed a way for her to put the blood on herself. Luckily, you'd spent enough nights next to the guest room plumbing to know how frequently she uses the bathroom late at night. Downstairs, you emptied the soap bottle, and then used a syringe to fill it with Pearse's blood. Somewhere along the way you dropped the lightbulb, and you had to clean it up, of course. Because a regular smashed wineglass would fit the scene, but a lightbulb would have people looking at the empty socket upstairs. All that's left is to simply put the pump-action soap bot-tle back in the bathroom. Erin gets up in the middle of the night, tries to flick the light on and gets no result, and so uses the bath-room in the dark, so she can't see it's not soap. You got the idea from when you and some other graduates dyed Flick's hair blue by swapping her shampoo. It's the same trick. Unbeknownst to Erin, she washes her hands in her dead boyfriend's blood. It's as gross as it is genius."

I took a breath. We were now halfway over the gorge. Still it was only theories I was spouting. Correct ones, I assure you, but legally, in order to exonerate Erin, I needed him to confess. Or shoot me. I had a distinct preference.

"You can't just rinse DNA off. You probably expected the wa-ter to wash most of the blood away, and the trace of it only to show up forensically when police checked her hands. But soap is more evaporative than blood, it washes off easier, so Erin proba-bly thought she was clean when she'd really just spread it around. And the kicker? It was a hot night. Erin splashed her face and arms, unknowingly coating herself further, and let the water air-dry for the coolness. She flicked her hands dry, which is why there are flecks on the bathroom tiles. She doesn't touch the light switch on the way out: Why would she? There's no blood on the switch, which at first had me thinking she'd gotten bloody later, but she only touched it once on her way in. She went into the bathroom bloodless and came out bloodied. She just didn't know it."

I swear the Cable Car had slowed down. The opposite cliffside seemed forever away.

"You just had to wait until she'd gone back to sleep, and then sneak off with the soap bottle. I'm sure Sullivan will find it in the bush somewhere, about as far as you could hurl it. Then you turned your attention to Rylan. You believed in the foundation, you said it saved your life. And you believe in second chances. You couldn't watch five people, four of whom were under your direct care, go through with a conspiracy to commit murder. You decided to give them a second chance. If you killed Rylan first, you'd make them all innocent. And maybe you'd learned enough about Rylan along the way that it didn't bother you as much as you thought it would.

"We know how you did it, of course. Shaun had plotted most of it out for you. You just added the final touches. The piece he couldn't figure out: using a real blade would make it impossible to look like an accident, which is why he decided on the bullets instead. Theresa told me she'd turned to break-and-enters and knew firsthand about glass. But that applies to anyone who's broken a window, it's not evidence. Then I remembered the Academy Award trophy in Lyle's office, the one you gave him as thanks. It's expertly crafted. I thought Flick was talking about the message on it—*It Was Worth It*—when she suggested it was a good reminder to you too. But she was talking about the figurine itself. She meant it was a reminder of your talent. You made the figurine. That means it wasn't humility that had you shying away from Flick's compliments about your arts scholarship, it was because you didn't want me to know that your artistic specialty was glass. I must admit to some prejudice here: I thought the thermal burns on your fingers were from drug use, but they are from molten glasswork, aren't they? You had all the skills to craft and implement the guillotine blade. And everything you needed was in the workshop. The only thing that went wrong was me causing a fuss onstage about the bullets. You were banking on a few moments of it seeming like an accident so you could slip under the stage and clean up. Tada! An invisible and disappearing blade. My antics ruined that for you."

Christopher gave me a sad smile. "You've got it all right, except one thing. I didn't kill Lyle because of any of that. I might have, eventually. But I killed him because . . ." He shook his head minutely. "Because he flinched."

"He *flinched*?"

"In his kitchen. I reached for my phone, and he flinched. Like I was trying to hit him, or steal something. And I saw that, no matter what I gave the foundation, he always saw the old me. The shivering, addicted boy. He didn't believe I was *me*." His lip trembled. "I don't know whether I meant to kill him or not, but the knife was in my hand and he was on the ground, and there was blood, and he was about to scream and . . . it was all so quick. I honestly don't remember it happening. I thought he was dead instantly. I almost ran, but I keep a first aid kit in my car and it gave me an idea. When I got back, he'd written out that message in his own blood. Rylan was . . ." His voice darkened. "Easier."

"Half of that's a lie. This is an organized and methodical plan. You went there knowing you might kill him," I said. "But you can convince yourself that you acted on impulse, if it makes you feel better. Don't they teach disassociation in psychology anymore?"

Christopher trembled. "For all your airs of cleverness, it was a stupid idea to make it so we're alone together." He waved the gun at the glass walls. "What you've just told me can't leave here. *You* brought the gun, after all. Yes. Don't you see? You threatened me. Desperate to pin some insane story on me to clear your ex-wife's name." His voice changed to mock discovery. "I was lucky to get the gun off you. Did what I had to. To protect myself, you understand?"

"No one will believe—"

He waved a hand. "They will. You know, until now, I didn't think of myself as a murderer." He tilted the gun at me. "But I think I'm getting the hang of it."

"You get that?" I spoke into my backpack. From one of the side pockets I pulled a device that looked like a circuit board crossed with a cockroach. It was a listening device and a GPS tracker, the one Josh had planted in my car. That was how he'd managed to pop up everywhere I was—from traffic court to Katoomba—and it was also why, after I'd yelled in impotent rage at my steering wheel, he'd clasped his ear and winced. At the time, I'd thought he was concussed, but in reality I'd just blown the noise levels on his headset.

Of course, I hadn't told Josh I'd found his bug, but he'd have figured it out by now. There's his exclusive.

"Everyone's listening," I said. Through the window I saw the dock coming closer. We'd be there in thirty seconds. Better still, I had the confession, so Christopher didn't have to shoot me for Erin to be off the hook.

He did it anyway. Square in the chest.

CHAPTER 26

Despite being shot, I narrate this not as a ghost of Christmas past, present or future.

The wax bullet inside the gun had done what I'd hoped it would: dissipated in the air. I told you my life depended on the fact that Theresa would do anything to protect her sister. I'd been right. Sam may have switched the bullets backstage. But, during the show, Theresa had switched them back.

Twins aren't supposed to switch in a mystery, unless you give fair warning. I did tell you they would switch. In a way.

I'm not an idiot. I wouldn't bet my life on my own deductions. While I couldn't open the gun to confirm the ammunition inside, I had found the real bullet—without the W etched onto its base, that Rylan had palmed to Shaun during the show—in the workshop. Knowing what was outside the gun told me what was inside it. I held the real bullet up to brag about my cleverness, as it is the detective's right to do in a finale, but no sound came out.

I tried again. No gloating, only a gurgle.

Any satisfaction I had was quickly replaced by a pain in my chest. I looked down and saw blood soaking my shirt. I thought back to Theresa, pulling Sam away from the gun even when she knew it was a wax bullet. I remembered the dotted line on the schematic: the minimum safe distance before the wax dissolved. Before that distance, it was pretty much a real bullet.

I staggered and felt the second bullet slide in my fingers, but my muscles refused to close that hand. It fell, tinkled on the glass floor. Christopher dropped to his knees after it. I looked out the window. I heard the gun click: unlocked, having been fired, and reloaded. The cliffside was getting closer, but it was fuzzy in my vision now.

Christopher stood up. He registered the blood on my shirt with a chuckle and then lifted the gun. I tried to stay standing, I didn't want to die on my knees, but my legs were shaking. I held my still-working arm out in front of me like a flimsy shield. Then Christopher looked back to the dock: Flick, Shaun and Dinesh watching it all unfold. Others arriving. Uniforms. Christopher's knuckle went white on the trigger. But then, slowly, he lowered the gun and his head at the same time. Had I been able to breathe at all—any breath I could take was wet and strange, I could taste blood—my sigh of relief would have been short-lived. Christopher fired anyway. Straight down, into the glass floor.

The bullet bounced off with a *chink*, leaving a chip in the glass.

The dock was only twenty-five meters away but it may as well have been a football field. The sheer drop of the cliffside meant we were still hundreds of meters in the air. With a sound like the tearing of sticky tape, a crack shot out from the chip, racing toward the corners like a jagged bolt of lightning. Then another. Then everywhere at once, until the whole floor was a spiderweb of cracks.

"Merry Christmas, I suppose," Christopher said, smug.

The glass floor gave way beneath us.

EPILOGUE

Slapdash Sleuth Throws Killer from Cable Car.

Juliette read the Christmas Day headline aloud from my laptop and rubbed my shoulder.

The lead photo was a doozy: Christopher was midair underneath the now-bottomless Cable Car, and I dangled by my good arm from the handrailing inside the cabin. When the Cable Car had finally pulled into the dock I was clutching on by fingertips alone.

As for being shot: turns out I'd been far enough away to only cop a third of the wax bullet. A punctured lung was my reward.

"You'd think Felman'd finally write something nice about you," Juliette continued. I scrolled the article. Dinesh, Sam, Theresa and Shaun were assisting with inquiries. Because the bullets hadn't hurt anyone, it was difficult to charge them with conspiracy. As the only one who'd committed a verifiable crime, Flick had been arrested. Christopher had, bizarrely, succeeded in giving all his graduates a second chance. "Given everything that happened."

"He is my nemesis," I offered. "I'd be disappointed if it was anything other than bad press."

"I can't believe you thought Erin was hypnotized." Juliette had been sitting in an armchair reading each chapter as I wrote it, so she was up to the epilogue. "What a cop-out that would have been."

"Excuse you!" I playfully swatted her away. "I think I did quite well actually, given I had to adhere to both the rules of mysteries *and* Holiday Specials."

"And what exactly are the rules for Holiday Specials?"

"I don't know." I shrugged. "I might have to write them."

"How about," Juliette suggested, looking again at my near-death dangling, "no more murders until after the wedding? Actually, don't make promises you can't keep. Oh, before I forget."

She handed me a present, wrapped in gold paper. I read the label. *To Ernest, Merry Christmas. From: Secret Santa.* I shook the box. It felt a little light.

"I might open this one last," I said.

Ernest Cunningham's 7 Commandments of Holiday Specials

1. With respect to everyone's holiday plans, the crime must be committed within a finite window. Preferably after December 20 and solved by New Year's Eve, with the exception of certain serial killers, who may conduct their sprees from December 1 for the purposes of "countdown to Christmas" thrillers.

2. The killer must not hate Christmas or have had a traumatic experience involving Christmas: for the purposes of a Christmas mystery, the "Grinch" is too predictable.

3. The detective must, at some point, learn the true meaning of the word *Christmas*.

4. The Holiday Special may be considered canon, but not required reading. As such, no major character deaths or series-long plot arcs may be introduced or resolved, with the exception of returning characters thought to be dead from earlier in the series, for the purposes of fan service nostalgia, who may be introduced in flashbacks, dream sequences, hypnosis or drug-induced hallucinations.

5. In either the costuming, weaponry or the method of murder, there must be a Christmas theme.

6. The full cast of the series is not required. Select cameos suffice.

7. All the regular rules of mystery writing apply. No exceptions just because it's the holidays.

ACKNOWLEDGMENTS

Despite being set among real locations, the Pearse Foundation, those involved with it, and the issues they face are products of my imagination and don't represent any particular community. The Blue Mountains are far better thought of for their natural beauty than they are for labyrinthine murder plots. I also have nothing against magicians.

Thank you to Beverley Cousins, Katherine Nintzel and Grace Long, my publishers, for the unreserved enthusiasm for Christmas hijinks, and for making the impossible possible (by this I mean correcting my plots so the murders add up, but also just the fact I get to write books—what a dream). I am grateful for the indescribable amount of behind-the-scenes work by my agents: thank you to Pippa Masson, assisted by Caitlan Cooper-Trent, for books, and Leslie Conliffe, assisted by Kris Karcher, for film. I also will always owe thanks to Jerry Kalajian. Thank you Amanda Martin and Andrew Clarke for, as always, insightful editing, and to Hannah Ludbrook, Maureen Cole, Tavia Kowalchuk, Rachel Berquist, Jennifer Hart, Shannon McCain, Alison Smith, Tanaya Lowden, Adelaide Jensen, Hannah Armstrong, and Jennifer Harlow for pushing my books into so many people's hands, and to Kate Falkoff for the same but across oceans. Thank you to Richard Ljoenes and Jeanne Reina for the incredible covers, and to Jennifer Chung for the interiors: thanks for being fun and playful with ideas and designs.

Thank you to every bookseller who recommended *Everyone in My Family Has Killed Someone* or *Everyone on This Train Is a Suspect* over the last two years, and for again supporting this book with such passion and kindness. Thank you to every reader for solving puzzles with me, for sharing your guesses, casework and deductions. I am very lucky to have such passionate detectives as readers. I hope you had fun with this slightly shorter book. Don't worry: Ernest is back in a big way soon.

Lastly, and always, thank you to my supportive, welcoming family: Peter, Judy, Emily and James Stevenson; and Gabriel, Elizabeth, Lucy and Adrian Paz.

And Aleesha Paz. The recipe for any book is ink, paper, and you.

This book is set on the land of the Dharug and Gun-dungurra peoples, and was written on the land of the Gadigal people of the Eora Nation.

ABOUT THE AUTHOR

BENJAMIN STEVENSON is an award-winning stand-up comedian and *USA Today* bestselling author. He is the author of the globally popular Ernest Cunningham mysteries, including *Everyone in My Family Has Killed Someone*, which is currently being adapted into a major HBO TV series, and *Everyone on This Train Is a Suspect*. His books have sold more than 750,000 copies in twenty-nine territories and have been nominated for eight Book of the Year awards.

His latest mystery is *Everyone This Christmas Has a Secret*. His Instagram handle is @stevensonexperience.

ABOUT MARINER BOOKS

MARINER BOOKS traces its beginnings to 1832 when William Ticknor cofounded the Old Corner Bookstore in Boston, from which he would run the legendary firm Ticknor and Fields, publisher of Ralph Waldo Emerson, Harriet Beecher Stowe, Nathaniel Hawthorne, and Henry David Thoreau. Following Ticknor's death, Henry Oscar Houghton acquired Ticknor and Fields and, in 1880, formed Houghton Mifflin, which later merged with venerable Harcourt Publishing to form Houghton Mifflin Harcourt. HarperCollins purchased HMH's trade publishing business in 2021 and reestablished their storied lists and editorial team under the name Mariner Books.

Uniting the legacies of Houghton Mifflin, Harcourt Brace, and Ticknor and Fields, Mariner Books continues one of the great traditions in American bookselling. Our imprints have introduced an incomparable roster of enduring classics, including Hawthorne's *The Scarlet Letter*, Thoreau's *Walden*, Willa Cather's *O Pioneers!*, Virginia Woolf's *To the Lighthouse*, W.E.B. Du Bois's *Black Reconstruction*, J.R.R. Tolkien's *The Lord of the Rings*, Carson McCullers's *The Heart Is a Lonely Hunter*, Ann Petry's *The Narrows*, George Orwell's *Animal Farm* and *Nineteen Eighty-Four*, Rachel Carson's *Silent Spring*, Margaret Walker's *Jubilee*, Italo Calvino's *Invisible Cities*, Alice Walker's *The Color Purple*, Margaret Atwood's *The Handmaid's Tale*,

Tim O'Brien's *The Things They Carried*, Philip Roth's *The Plot Against America*, Jhumpa Lahiri's *Interpreter of Maladies*, and many others. Today Mariner Books remains proudly committed to the craft of fine publishing established nearly two centuries ago at the Old Corner Bookstore.